KNIGHTS OF THE DEAD GOD

JAMES JAKINS

For Daniel. The next one will have dragons. I promise.

ARRIVAL

WE ENTERED the world in a flash of fire and thunder. It is no small thing to tear your way into a new dimension. The fall through the darkness and light had felt like it had lasted forever, and when we finally exploded through the fabric of reality, with my first breath in an eternity, I cried.

I was only six years old and it felt like the natural thing to do at the time. The screaming monster still attached to the old man helped with that decision, as well.

It had fallen with us, through the space between things, silent, but always visible. Claws and teeth unable to move closer, just as I was unable to move farther away.

But now, now it could move.

Its mouth snapped open and closed, teeth just inches from the man's face as he pushed it back away from himself.

Claws gripped the old man's forearms, and I watched in growing horror as the blood pooled in the black fabric of the man's shirt.

With a final grunt of effort, the man pushed the monster back, its too-human face twisting in surprise at the burst of strength. There was the quiet sound of steel rasping against leather and the man held a sword.

The sword was broken, even as a child I could tell that. At some time in its history the point had been shattered away, and now the double-edged blade was topped with an uneven tip.

But it was sharp. Sharp enough for the work of killing.

I cried louder as the blade entered the monster's neck and black, acrid blood poured out onto the leaf-covered ground of the forest.

I covered my face and curled up on the ground. I cried for my mother, my father, my Uncle Jack, my dead grandmother, for anyone that might be able to save me from the nightmare I was living. But the only person there was Arthur.

I felt a shaking hand on my shoulder and I instinctively flinched away.

"It's okay." The old man knelt over me. "It's gone now. My name's Arthur. What's yours?"

I could tell that he wasn't used to talking with children, and his words felt forced, even to me, but the fact that he was trying calmed me a little.

"Where's my mom?" I demanded of him.

His face fell a little as he glanced around. The lines of age deepening around his eyes and mouth. "She's safe. I'm sure of that. My friends are still with her." He avoided looking at me for a time as he studied the red and brown of the trees around us. "Where we are is probably a more important question."

I echoed his statement with the question. "Where are we?" I rose to my feet and wiped my running nose on the sleeve of my winter coat.

Without really meaning to, I turned from the color of

the fall trees to the dead thing on the ground. I could feel the sobs begin again.

Before the first one broke free I was interrupted by the group of riders that rounded a corner of the road I hadn't noticed us standing near.

Arthur stepped between me and the road, sword held at his side.

The group of riders stopped on the road in front of us and the nearest man shouted at us in a language I didn't understand.

Arthur let out a surprised breath and stepped toward them, shouting something in the same language.

Several of the riders raised crossbows and shouted at Arthur. He froze in mid-step. He spoke again, his tone calmer, and he made a show of deliberately sheathing his sword.

Most of the riders lowered their weapons at this, but one maintained his shot and spoke again.

Arthur answered and the two spoke for a short time. Fingers were pointed at me, Arthur, the dead thing on the ground. Arthur answered all questions with a calm, patient tone.

I stepped closer and peered around Arthur's leg at the group.

One of the riders noticed me and smiled. The woman seemed young, but I recognized the pointed ears. This was an elf. I stared up in awe. I'd only ever known one elf in my six long years of life and she was someone I'd always admired.

The woman climbed down from her horse, and after asking Arthur something in their strange language, approached and squatted down in front of me.

She spoke again, directly at me. I shook my head, hoping she understood that I didn't understand her.

"She's asking for your name," Arthur translated for me.

"Miki," I turned to her and said.

"Miki," she repeated. She held a hand to her chest and said, "Lara."

I grinned at that.

The woman stepped back in surprise and turned to Arthur, demanding something of him.

Arthur knelt and stared at me. I balked at the attention.

"What is your family name, child?" Arthur asked, trying to keep his voice calm.

"What?" I stared at him, confused at the sudden interest my smile had created.

"Last name," he clarified.

"Goretusk," I answered.

The elf woman turned to her friends and began to shout something while pointing at me.

Arthur lowered his head at that. "You are Shakill's granddaughter." It wasn't a question.

"Yes." I glanced from Arthur to the now very animated group of riders.

Arthur gave me a reassuring smile before rising and turning to face the riders.

He spoke for a while, the only words I could understand were his name, Arthur Shield. His name created a reaction even more pronounced than mine.

After his short speech, the elf woman, Lara, nodded her head and indicated her horse.

Arthur turned back to me and, before I could protest, lifted me off the ground. "These people are going to take us somewhere safe. Okay?"

I was still too shocked to argue and simply nodded.

Arthur placed me on the horse and climbed up to sit behind me. He leaned forward and whispered in my ear. "Try not to show anyone your teeth if you can help it. Orcs are not very popular here."

I turned in my seat and stared up at him. "Why not?"

Arthur shook his head. "It doesn't matter. Just hold on tight."

At that he kicked the horse and it took off, keeping pace with the other riders, all of whom were studying me with wary glances or openly hostile glares.

The elf had climbed on another horse and watched me the entire ride. Her scrutiny felt like a hole burning through my skull.

———

The ride took several hours and before the first had even passed I was ready to cry from the pain. I held it in though. I did cry about being separated from my parents. I tried to keep it quiet, but with the constant attention from the surrounding riders, I'm sure everyone noticed.

Every so often Arthur would say something to one of the other riders and they would respond.

At the point where I was sure I couldn't take any more of the saddle, Arthur spoke and all the riders stopped.

He climbed down from the saddle and lifted me off. Setting me on the ground he squatted down next to me. "How are you holding up, Miki?"

I sniffed and wiped my nose again before answering. "I'm okay. I miss my mom."

He nodded. "I know. We're going to do our best to get you back to her, okay? I have some friends that should be able to help with that. We'll be there soon. Can you ride for just a little longer?"

I nodded again. The prospect of riding any more was not one I liked, but if he thought it would get me back home faster, then I was more than willing to give it another shot.

He put me back on the horse and we rode some more.

Eventually the trees thinned and the dirt road became a paved one. Rolling grassland gave way to fenced fields of golden wheat or grazing sheep. A small village appeared after we crested a small hill and I marveled at the simple one-room buildings and their thatched roofs.

One stone-walled building stood two stories high, dwarfing everything around it. A sign swung over the door with a picture of a laughing pig holding a foaming mug.

Once in town several of the riders turned off and rode toward what I assumed were their homes. Lara, the elf, and the man she shared her horse with remained with Arthur and me until we reached the stone building.

Once more Arthur removed me from the horse and set me on the ground. He turned from me and had a short exchange with Lara.

The elf was animated as she whispered the angriest whispers I'd ever heard. Arthur calmly nodded and replied to each of her statements.

Finally, as she was in mid-sentence with something that seemed especially toxic, Arthur simply handed her the reigns to her horse and turned away from her. Without consulting me, he bent down and picked me up. I didn't argue as he rested me on his shoulder and made his way inside the building.

From over his shoulder I watched Lara and her friend as they glared back at us before she climbed on her horse and they rode away.

Inside was warm and smoky. A fire burned in a large fireplace against one wall. There was a sour smell in the air that reminded me of my grandmother, as well as the warm scents of bread and cooking meat. The room was full of tables and benches, about half of which were occupied by tired looking people. Some looked up at our entrance, but most seemed too preoccupied with their own lives to care about the intrusion of any strangers.

"Remember," he whispered, "keep your mouth shut."

I frowned down at him, but he ignored my displeasure.

He sat me down on a bench at one of the empty tables and approached a rough-looking man standing behind a bar against one of the walls.

I turned from Arthur and studied the rest of the room. The long ride had managed to calm me, and I was starting to be very curious about this strange place that reminded me of a cartoon I'd seen once.

A pretty woman sitting on the next table over noticed my attention and smiled at me. I almost smiled back but remembered Lara's reaction and lowered my head, embarrassed. The elf must have seen my tusks. They were small, nothing like some of my cousins', but sometimes I wished I didn't have them. They were small enough that my orc cousins always made fun of me, but big enough that my human cousins were afraid of me. Too human or too orc. It was a painful place to be for a little girl.

The bench next to me groaned under added weight and I looked up to find the woman over me. "Hi, my name's Hazel, what's yours?" she said in perfect English.

I stared up at her, still afraid to open my mouth, but relief filled me that someone else spoke a language I could understand.

"It's okay. I don't bite, I promise."

7

While she spoke, Arthur approached from behind and tilted his head as he studied her. "You speak English."

She jumped a little at his tone and turned to study him. "Excuse me?" she said.

He sat down across from her and his gaze went from me to her. "Where did you learn that language?" he demanded.

She answered quickly. "I've always had a good ear for languages. I just picked it up somewhere."

"Hm." Arthur considered her for a moment then spoke again, this time in the strange tongue he and the riders had used. The woman answered in the same language.

Arthur grinned, humorously. "That's what I thought."

I looked at Hazel and found her face paling. "I slipped back into Imperial, didn't I?"

Arthur nodded. "So, what are you?"

"I'm nobody," Hazel insisted, as she pushed to her feet.

"Sit down, it's fine. If I'd met you a year ago I might have cared, but in that time... well, some of my best friends are magic users. I'm guessing you cast some sort of language spell? Let's anyone understand you?"

Hazel sat back down. She was tense and studied Arthur with apprehension. "Yeah. I'm not really a witch or anything. I just know a few spells." Both were speaking quietly and anytime they mentioned magic in any way they would lean in closer and almost whisper the words.

"A spell of comprehension must be useful. Especially for a traveler. Where are you heading?" Arthur asked.

She opened her mouth to answer but froze when another figure approached the table. A girl, maybe sixteen or seventeen, smiled at all of us as she placed two plates on the table, one in front of me and one for Arthur.

She said something to Hazel and the woman answered with a shake of her head and a friendly smile.

Once the server was gone, Hazel answered Arthur. "I'm heading to Glanzend. I have family there."

Arthur picked up the chunk of bread on his plate and motioned to me that I should do the same. I did and began to devour the meal. The meat was tough, but I tore it apart with my teeth and sopped up the juices with the bread.

Arthur nodded, approving of my appetite, then turned his attention back to Hazel as he, with a little more restraint, ate his own meal. "Glanzend isn't the safest for someone with your...gift. What's your reason for traveling there?"

"I told you. I have family." She avoided his eye.

"Of course. Are you taking the carriage from here? I'm told it's arriving in a few hours."

"That was my plan."

"Traveling alone?"

I glanced up in time to catch her face change color again. This time her cheeks burned crimson. "So what if I am?"

"How are you with children?" he asked.

She considered Arthur for a moment before slowly turning to look back at me. "You looking to hire a nanny for your daughter?"

"She's not my daughter." He answered her the same time I blurted out, "He's not my dad!"

She quickly raised a placating hand toward each of us. "Sorry, sorry. But, you need..." she studied him as he nodded his answer to her unfinished question.

"I'm trying to get her home. My best chance for that is in the capital. I can't actually pay, but a young woman probably shouldn't be traveling the road alone. I'd be happy to help with your trip in whatever way I can."

She turned full to me. "Are you far from home?"

I looked at Arthur. "I don't know. Am I?"

"Incredibly."

"I don't know." Hazel kept studying me as I stared back, grease running down my chin. "Where are you two from, anyway?" she asked, finally. "You're both wearing some unusual clothing."

"I'm originally from Glanzend," Arthur said. "But I was in her homeland." He paused, considering his next words. "Some powerful magic sent us here. I have friends in the capital that should be able to help me get her back to her family. But, if at all possible, I would appreciate someone else who can speak to her. Someone with actual experience with children." He gave Hazel an almost pleading look.

"Really good at sidestepping questions, aren't you?" She never looked away from me.

"What was your name, sweetie, you never told me."

Arthur gave me the barest of nods and I answered. "Miki."

"Do you want me to travel with you, Miki?" she asked.

"How long before I'm home?" I asked Arthur.

"A few days on the road. Then it shouldn't be long."

I started to tear up as I met Hazel's eyes and nodded. "Please."

The thick wooden door flew open and banged against the stone wall. Lara the elf stood framed in the doorway. She was surrounded by a large group of people, men and women, all looked angry, and all were dressed in the same studded leather armor, weapons bared.

Lara's dark eyes scanned the room and rested on our table. She pointed directly at us and began to shout. I understood only a few words. My family name, Goretusk. And the word orc.

The tables around us began to empty as people rushed

to get out of the way. They pressed themselves up against the wall or hid behind the bar.

The innkeeper shouted something at her, but she silenced him with a few words.

Hazel's eyes widened, and she leaned in close and whispered in my ear. "Are you an orc, sweetie?"

I nodded as tears poured down my face.

Hazel clenched her jaw. "Okay. You stay close to me." She looked to Arthur, who was slowly rising from his seat, still finishing his bread. "What are you going to do? We have to get her out of here."

He wiped the crumbs off his hand on the black tactical vest he still wore and nodded. "Keep her safe, please."

Hazel wrapped her arms around me and pulled me under the table with her. "It's going to be okay, Miki. I promise." She pulled a small bag from somewhere and pulled out a thin, white stick about as long as her pinky finger.

Arthur Shield stepped around the table, standing between us and the intruders. He spoke softly, his tone very different from the friendly, warm demeanor he'd had until now.

The elf barked a command and her friends charged.

———

Arthur Shield doesn't draw his sword. Just waits. Waits as the armed intruders charge him, their own weapons ready to kill.

The first to reach him swings a spike tipped club, one made by no professional craftsman. By the time the club's overhead arc reaches its target the old man is not there. He has stepped, gracelessly, aside to allow the weapon free passage through the air.

Arthur grabs the back of the man's head with one hand and drives it forward into his elbow. There is the crack of breaking cartilage and the sudden coppery scent of blood.

As the man stumbles from his injury the old warrior twists a hand in the man's shirt and jerks him to the side. The man stumbles into one of his comrades, the second attacker's own notched sword being pulled back just in time. The two tangle and, with just a little help from Shield, they are both on the ground.

Arthur walks past them, sparing enough energy to casually kick the second man in the throat. The sound of angry cries replaced with rasping, choked breaths.

The first man tries to rise, blood from his nose absorbing into the sawdust of the inn floor. He is pushed back to the ground by the body of another of his friends, the woman wailing and grasping at an arm that is bent at an unnatural angle.

Shield dodges more attacks, more cheaply made weapons swung by inexperienced arms. He catches a hand holding a rusty dagger and punches into the wielder's arm. The weapon is dropped. Arthur catches it with his free hand and drives the point into the attacker's shoulder before sweeping their feet out from under them.

He is in the midst of them now. Completely surrounded with seemingly no way to move or dodge. But he finds ways. He is an old man. An old man that has spent a lifetime avoiding death. He ducks and dodges, sidesteps and strafes. He catches arms and throws his opponents into each other. He takes advantage of their confidence and inexperience.

As he ducks under a swung staff he scoops a dented pewter mug from a table. The weak foam of heavily watered beer explodes up and out as the mug crumples against the side of a head.

He kicks out a foot with just the right pressure and another pained scream joins the chorus as a kneecap breaks.

He continues this way. Picking up dinnerware or chairs or disarming. Using his hands and feet he breaks noses and arms and legs.

Before very long at all, he stands at the doorway before the elf, Lara, a trail of groaning or crying men and women behind him.

"Now," he addresses the elf as she stares, eyes wide in shock, "was there something you wished to discuss, madam elf?"

Her lips peel back in a snarl and she is on him, using fists and teeth she attacks. With a feral leap she wraps her legs around his torso and begins to swing.

He manages to get his arms up but her attacks reopen not-yet-healed wounds and blood again soaks into his clothing.

He grimaces and lets out a pained yelp as her teeth dig into the flesh of one hand.

He throws his arms and returns her embrace. With a grunt, he squeezes.

She gasps at the sudden pressure and loosens her own grip on him. He grabs her sides and pushes. Fabric tears as she grasps his shirtsleeves.

Then his forehead finds her nose and her head rocks back. With eyes watering and blood pouring from her destroyed nose she completely loses her grip.

He throws her to the ground.

"Fine. No talk." He guides a heavy boot into the side of her head and she stops moving.

He studies the blood pouring freely down his arm with

a small level of distaste before looking up at the gathered crowd.

"Someone, call your village healer. That one, at least, really needs help." He points to a man, red faced, struggling to breath.

GRANNIE SUMMER

It ended as quickly as it started. I didn't see most of it, since Hazel had her hand over my face, but I saw the end as Arthur kicked Lara in the side of the head and her body went limp. I saw him turn and address the crowd.

No one said anything at first, not until a small, wiry man rushed out the door after being yelled at by a large woman I assumed was his wife.

Then the crowd began to shout and yell. Arthur's expression never changed. He simply strode up to our table and motioned for Hazel to bring me out.

She did so and then he placed a softly shaking hand on the woman's shoulder and led us outside.

"I would understand if you'd rather not travel with us now." Arthur said to Hazel after we were outside.

She was silent as she held me, but she followed him down the road a short way. I mostly ignored the two of them as I watched the wiry man return to the inn with a short old woman in tow.

"Is she really a Goretusk?" Hazel said finally, after

Arthur had stopped in front of a bench under a small awning.

Arthur looked at me before answering. I simply sat in a shocked silence. "She is."

"Who are you that you would travel with, let alone protect, an orc girl?" Hazel was still holding the small white stick and was now aiming it at Arthur.

He seemed to notice the item and raised his hands as though she held a gun. "That doesn't matter. But I owe it to her family to get her home."

"And how does Glanzend get her home? I know what they do to orcs in Glanzend."

"What do they do to orcs in Glazen?" I asked.

Hazel stared down at me in horror, as though just realizing I could hear her.

"Nothing. They won't do anything to you as long as you're with me," Arthur reassured me.

"Who are you?" Hazel said again, her tone pleading now.

Arthur sighed. "Promise you won't do anything stupid."

"What?" Hazel waved the stick. "Why?"

"Please put the wand away. I don't want to have to hurt you, Miss."

"Hazel," Hazel blurted out. "My name's Hazel Midd." She didn't lower the stick, which I was now studying intently. It didn't look like any wand I'd ever seen, just a sun-bleached twig.

"Okay. I don't want to hurt you, Miss Midd. Please put the weapon away." His tone was so calm that I felt like putting a weapon away and I didn't even have one.

Slowly the wand was lowered and disappeared in the folds of Hazel's traveling cloak.

"Thank you. My name is Arthur Shield. I was once a paladin of Saban."

Hazel's movement was fast. Before either Arthur or I could register it, the wand was back in her hands and aimed at the old man's face. "You get away from us." She held me tighter to her side as she slowly began to back away.

"Do you really think I mean you or the girl any harm? Didn't you see what I did in there?" Arthur indicated the inn down the road. People were now exiting the building and staring toward us.

Hazel considered them before turning back to Arthur. "I don't know. But I wouldn't trust any child to the care of one of Saban's dogs."

"So, you want her? You want to take the girl?" Arthur asked. He sighed again and shook his head. "Are you still going to Glanzend? Alone?"

Hazel hesitated in her retreat to consider me. "Where's your family, Miki? Maybe I can take you to them."

My eyes filled with the tears that had just been waiting. "Summervale," I said.

Hazel looked confused. "Where is that?"

I shook my head, confused by the question.

"Another world, Miss Midd." Arthur hadn't moved toward us. "On the other side of the very fabric of existence."

Hazel's eyes were wide with fear and confusion. "What?"

"But, please. Take the girl. It would make my life easier. And don't worry. I won't tell anyone in Glanzend of the witch or the half-orc child." He turned away from Hazel and sat back down on the bench.

"Another world?" Hazel asked softly. She looked into my tear-filled eyes and repeated the question.

I nodded. I vaguely knew the story of where my family had come from. Another world, I'd always been told. So, I knew it was possible that now I wasn't in the same one. And Arthur seemed so sure of that. I believed him. As much as I could believe anything, I believed that.

Hazel considered me, then the growing crowd of people. Some were pointing at her now and she seemed to realize she was still pointing her wand at Arthur. She quickly returned it to her cloak and hurried us back to the bench.

She hesitated before sitting down next to Arthur. "You swear you mean me no harm?"

Arthur didn't look at her as he answered. "I told you. I don't want to hurt anyone. Besides," he looked at her with the vague shadow of a smile turning his lips upward, "One of my best friends is a young witch. In the years since I left Glanzend, I've come to learn that a lot of what I believed was wrong. I regret much of it. Returning this girl home will be one way of making amends for some of that."

"But you still intend to return to your order?" There was an excess of bitterness in that question.

Arthur nodded. "If it still stands, yes."

"It does." Anger flooded with the bitterness.

Arthur didn't seem to miss the tone. "I see."

The three of us sat in silence for a while.

"So," Arthur said, finally. "Do you have any baggage you need help with? The cart should be arriving before too long."

Hazel shook her head. "Even if I did, I'm not heading back into that inn." She eyed the massing crowd that was still watching us with something akin to fear.

"Understandable. And what of my earlier offer? Are you against helping an old man?"

Hazel smiled down at me and gave me another warm squeeze. "I'll come along for Miki."

I returned the smile and allowed myself to be lost in the embrace.

———

Before the cart arrived, we were visited by a group of armed men. They approached cautiously, seemingly trying not to alarm us.

Arthur spoke with them in that strange language. I glanced up at Hazel and asked, "What are they saying?"

Hazel seemed to consider answering before telling me. "They're the local guard. They're asking about what happened at the inn. Master Shield is explaining who he is. They don't seem to believe that he really is a paladin."

"What's a Palldin?"

"Paladin," she corrected. "It means he's a servant of a god. A warrior that fights for whatever his god tells him to." The bitterness in her voice returned.

"Oh." I'd heard the word before that day. I knew I had, but I couldn't remember where, or in what context.

Hazel went back to listening to Arthur speaking. "You have got to be kidding me," she said under her breath.

"What?" I asked.

"They just gave him a bag of coin and wished him luck on his travels... I guess he convinced them." She turned back to me and said, in the tone of a teacher, "The Order of Saban has a lot of influence with law enforcement in the empire. I guess they take the God of Justice thing seriously."

I really didn't understand but I was relieved that Arthur wouldn't have to fight again.

The armored men had brought a woman with them.

Hazel and I watched as she rolled his sleeve back and winced at the sight of the ragged wound on his arm. The blood had clotted, but it still looked terrible. She said something, her tone insistent, but Arthur simply shook his head.

With a sigh that reminded me of my mother any time I refused to eat my vegetables, the woman nodded her head reluctantly. She fished around in a large satchel hanging at her side and pulled out a jar and a roll of white cloth. She handed both to Arthur and seemed to be giving him instructions.

He bowed his head and accepted the items gratefully.

He watched the guards and the woman leave before returning to the bench and sitting back down. He offered the two of us a tired smile. "Went better than I expected."

"You didn't have any money, did you?" Hazel seemed to realize. She was eyeing the small leather pouch that Arthur held in his lap with the jar and bandages the woman had given him.

"None that would be accepted here."

"How were you planning on getting onto the cart without paying for your ticket?"

He shrugged. "I had faith things would work out."

"Oh, so Saban provided?" She winced slightly at her own tone.

Arthur's face darkened and he scowled at the young woman. "No."

"I'm sorry, I shouldn't have said it like that. I'm sure he takes care of his followers..." she reluctantly conceded.

Arthur shook his head. "It's fine. But it wasn't Saban. Not directly. I did use my former position in the order to get them to agree to not press charges about what happened, but I think it was more that they wanted us gone before

Lara and her friends recovered enough to try again." He still seemed upset and fell into a sullen silence.

Hazel looked away and seemed to shrink into herself. "I'm sorry, Master Shield. I would understand if you changed your mind about traveling with me."

Arthur didn't look at her when he finally answered. "What did the order do to you, Miss Midd? You have an obvious dislike for them."

She seemed taken aback by the directness of the question. "Nothing to me."

"Someone you know, then? They pronounced a justice you were unhappy with?"

She shook her head. "It doesn't matter."

"It does if you really want to travel with us. You obviously dislike me. Even if you claim it is just for the girl, you obviously need something from me. My connections? Is it to avoid suspicion in the city? Must be risky for a witch in Glanzend."

It was again Hazel's turn to sit in silence before answering. "I mean no offense when I say this, Master Shield, but no, I don't like you. I've never met a paladin that I can say I like. And, again, no offense is intended, but I don't trust you. Not with my purpose for traveling to Glanzend, nor with the wellbeing of a child."

Arthur nodded at this. "I understand. I won't press the matter."

Neither of them spoke again. I just sat on the bench and considered the two of them in turn.

Arthur had rolled his sleeve up and was applying a pungent paste from the jar he'd been given directly to the wound on his arm, over the dried blood and the red, enflamed tears. Fresh blood mixed with the yellowish substance. Then he wrapped the wound in the white fabric.

Hazel was staring at her hands as she turned her twig sized wand over and over. Her mouth moved silently and she occasionally shook her head, face twisting as though she were arguing with herself and didn't like what she had to say.

The atmosphere felt a lot like whenever my parents had fought in front of me. They had been rare occasions, but I remembered them.

The most common fight had been about my grandmother before she died. Mom hadn't liked that her mother-in-law had been a criminal of some kind in the old country. She especially didn't like that the old orc woman liked to tell me stories about some of her more questionable accomplishments. My favorite had always been her story about when she had killed a troll. "A huge, rock-skinned thing, that troll," she always started the story.

"Had my brother under his foot and was ready to take his head off." She always paused the story to stick a finger in her mouth and make a popping sound. "So, I rushed in with my ax and saved my poor baby brother."

She had once told that story while my Uncle Jack was visiting for dinner. He'd seemed a little upset to hear that his dad had needed saving like that.

Mom always asked her to stop with the stories, and she would for a while, then she'd get the urge to tell another. And every time Mom would go to Dad and ask *him* to talk to her.

"I heard those same stories growing up, babe, and I turned out fine," he'd always counter.

Then Mom would start listing some of Dad's cousins who she didn't think had turned out fine and he'd get really quiet. Mom had once listed Uncle Jack and Dad actually shouted back.

Without completely understanding why, I started crying. Soft sobs shook my shoulders and tears streamed freely down my face.

Hazel wrapped me up in a hug again and made soothing sounds while rocking the two of us back and forth on the bench.

Arthur grew uncomfortable and rose. He paced back and forth, occasionally glancing at me. His expression was concerned, but I suspected it was more that he didn't like crying. This made me want to stop, but I couldn't.

Eventually I fell asleep, my head resting on Hazel's lap. I went in and out of wakefulness a few times. I could hear vague voices as Arthur and Hazel spoke, then I heard something moving on the road.

I woke up one more time to find myself lying on a cushioned seat, head still in Hazel's lap. She was staring out a small window. Outside the dirty glass I could see the moon and the occasional tree passing across its form. It looked wrong, somehow, but I couldn't place it right away. I bounced in my seat as the cart rode over something in the road.

I glanced around and found Arthur sitting at the other end of our cushioned bench. He was stretched out, his long legs in the aisle of the cart. Across from him was a figure I couldn't quite make out, asleep against their window.

Arthur must have sensed me studying him because he glanced down at me. His smile was weary as he acknowledged me with a small nod. Somehow that made me feel better about everything, and I fell back asleep.

———

I woke with sunlight on my face and sat up with a yawn and a cry ready to escape. For a time I forgot where I was. I expected to find my room, the smell of breakfast wafting in from downstairs. But I was sitting on a thin cushion in a bouncing cart.

I glanced up toward the window to find Hazel's face pressed against the glass with a small rivulet of drool flowing from the corner of her mouth. She snorted as the cart went over a particularly large bump in the road and readjusted herself against the window.

On my other side Arthur was sitting, arms crossed, and head bowed. His breathing was deep and rhythmic.

The sight of the two familiar faces—as familiar as anything in this strange world—helped calm me. I took a moment to study the rest of the cart.

I stood on my seat and looked around. It was bigger than I expected. Not quite as big as a school bus, but easily double the size of my mom's van. There was a row of benches running down either side of the vehicle. Most seemed to be occupied. I saw what I guessed to be a family far at the back. A man and woman dressed in raggedy clothing with a young boy and girl in their laps, their clothing even worse than the adults. The two children were grinning at each other as they each popped what appeared to be candy into their mouths.

Most of the passengers seemed to be asleep, and the whole vehicle was filled with the soft—occasionally loud—sound of snoring.

Looking to the front, I was surprised to see no driver. I wondered, correctly, if there was a man on the roof urging horses onward.

"First time on the cart?" a friendly voice asked.

I turned back around in my seat to find a friendly-faced

24

old woman staring up at me. She was short and round, not exactly fat, just plump in that way only old women can be. Her dress was faded and tattered at the fringes, the floral pattern barely visible.

I nodded shyly. I was still a little unsure of my surroundings and not comfortable with being as friendly as I usually was.

"Me too. Would you like some candy?" She held a shaking hand up. In her palm rested a waxy ball of paper.

I looked to my current guardians. Both seemed to still be asleep. I turned back to the woman and nodded.

"Well, go on, then." She raised her hand higher.

I reached out cautiously.

A large hand fell from above and enveloped my own. I looked up to find Arthur, half turned in his seat to stop me.

"What is your name, madam?" he asked the woman.

"You can call me Grannie Summer. What's your name, young man?"

"Arthur Shield." His tone was flat, emotionless, but his eyes were sharp as he stared at the old woman.

Grannie Summer's smile widened. I found myself afraid of that row of teeth. There were too many of them. They were too sharp.

"I know that name," she said.

"As you should. Now sit down, hag. This child is under my protection."

Without turning her head, Grannie's eyes moved from Arthur to me. "An orc child under the protection of one of Saban's knights? Well, now I have seen everything."

Arthur picked me up and sat me back in my seat as he spoke. "Return whatever potion you have to your bag if you wish to see anything else."

I sensed, more than heard, the old woman settle back

into her seat behind me. Arthur turned back around and faced forward. I felt like I was sitting next to a wound spring.

"Why—" I started to ask, but he raised a single finger and shook his head. I sat back and resigned myself to silence.

He and I both jumped when the old woman's face appeared over the seat between us. She smiled warmly at Arthur. "Might I, at least, ask how you knew?"

Arthur had a hand wrapped around the hilt of the large knife at his belt. The weapon was half-drawn before he took a deep breath and pushed it back inside. He scanned the cart. From what I could tell, no one else had noticed.

"Please?" Granny Summer asked.

"We're not speaking Imperial."

The old woman's eyes narrowed. "I see." Her head moved back and I could hear her making herself comfortable again.

Arthur reached over me and gently tapped Hazel's shoulder.

The woman sat up with a snort. She blinked at the old man through a tangle of hair. "Wha?"

"When's the next stop?" Arthur whispered as he leaned over me.

"Uh, I do'no. Where are we?" Hazel rubbed at her eyes as she yawned.

"Just coming up on Amethyst Lake." Grannie Summer leaned over the seat again. "Cart stops there. Should be arriving in the next hour."

Hazel blinked at the woman then turned back to Arthur. "There y'go." She turned back to the window and began to put her head against the glass.

"Hazel." Arthur's tone was still flat, but it got her attention.

"What?" She sat straight again and turned to consider him.

"We will be getting off at the next stop. Make sure you have all your things."

Hazel's eyes flashed and she was suddenly wide awake. She opened her mouth as though she were going to scream then glanced around. She leaned forward. "You know full well I had to leave all my stuff behind."

"Then we will replace what we can in town." Arthur leaned forward and with his hand well below the top of the seat he pointed behind us.

Hazel started to turn but Arthur let out a soft cough. When she looked back he simply nodded before sitting back down.

Hazel stared at him, confused for a moment before turning to face the front again. She sighed and closed her eyes. For a moment I thought she'd fallen asleep again, since her breathing had grown deep again, though it wasn't the snoring from earlier.

She opened her eyes and glanced at Arthur. She mouthed something I couldn't make out and the old man nodded. Hazel reached out and took my hand with one of her own, grasping it much more tightly than I thought was necessary.

I was about to ask her the question that Arthur had stopped earlier, but Hazel just squeezed my hand tighter and shook her head.

Both she and Arthur were studying the rest of the cart.

"I hope I'm not the reason you're disembarking so soon." The old woman was there again, leering over me.

"I ask that you remain in your seat, hag." This time the

knife did leave its sheath, though Arthur held it low, between his body and mine, hidden from the rest of the passengers.

"Now, why would you call a poor old woman that?" Her smile widened again, revealing even more pointed teeth.

Some of the other passengers began to stir. Either from the increasing brightness of the morning sun, or from the whispered confrontation on our bench.

Grannie Summer's eyes darted around the cart. They bulged from her face slightly, like a toad, as she, without turning her face, watched our neighbors.

I shrunk away from her and buried my face into Hazel's side.

"Oh, Sir Shield, you're frightening the girl." Grannie's voice grew louder, no longer even pretending to whisper.

Soon everybody in the cart was shifting and straightening in their seats.

"It's a shame you didn't just let her take the candy. You three were the last. Even the driver accepted my offer."

Arthur muttered a word my mother had warned me I was never supposed to say. "It doesn't matter if you heard Uncle Jack say it, Miki. It's a bad word."

I chose to focus on that memory rather than on what happened next.

———

"Fuck." Arthur can think of nothing better to say as the hag's eyes bulge farther and farther. As her grin stretches beyond the limits of her face.

He remembers a time when hags stayed in their swamps

or their deep woods. Remembers when they would never venture far from their walking houses.

Things have changed in the twenty years he has been away.

"They're all mine now, you see." The creature that calls herself Grannie Summer rises from her seat, moving into the aisle. Arthur does not fail to notice that her feet do not touch the ground.

Arthur's grip on his knife tightens. He wishes he had done something sooner. She offered the child candy. Only a hag would do that. Only a hag would somehow understand the girl from another world while offering sweets.

"You look frightened, Sir Shield." Grannie Summer looks around at the other passengers. "Doesn't he look scared?"

"Yes, Grannie Summer," everyone onboard intones, even the two children sitting in the back with their parents.

If Arthur were a younger man he might ask the crone, "Why?" He might ask her to release those she has taken through her foul magic. Might be thrown off by her initially frail appearance. Might even feel guilt at what he knows he has to do. But now, as an old man, he only regrets not slitting the monster's throat as soon as he realized what she was.

Before he is able to remedy his mistake, rough hands wrap around his legs, his arms, his throat. He is pulled from the bench and dragged into the aisle.

His knife flashes in the early morning sunlight. Even with the bumping of the cart his aim is sure. The man does not suffer. Not that there was still a man inside, but Arthur avoids that line of reasoning.

The passengers don't scream as they die. They simply collapse with blood pouring onto the wood of the floor.

One of the people clinging to Arthur sinks their teeth into his shoulder. Arthur is grateful for the vest he is still wearing, the bite only feels like pressure, but it helps him guide the next stab of the blade over his shoulder.

It sticks in the skull and is pulled out of his hand as the cart speeds up, gaining more air on the next bump. The body jerks, lodging the weapon.

Arthur almost drops after the weapon but forces himself to focus. He almost regrets stowing his sword under his bench, though he knows it would be worthless in the close quarters of the cart.

His mindless attackers are swinging fists and kicking at his legs.

He falls into a boxing stance and dances away from a fist thrown at his throat. He catches the arm and, with a grunt of effort, throws his own fist into the man's nose. There is an audible break as the man's face erupts in a fountain of blood.

Even completely under the hag's control, the body reacts to the damage and collapses on top of the others.

The space is confined, and Arthur is outnumbered. He knows that any betting man would bet against him. He is old and unarmed, after all. But, he is slightly embarrassed to admit to himself, this is not the first time he's been in this exact situation. There was no hag last time, of course, but he was on a bus alone against ten other men. And they had been professionals. These here are just the shallow husks of former farmers and craftsmen.

In the corner of his mind, he ignores the crying of the small girl.

Hazel Midd cradles the girl in one arm, thin stick held out in the other.

An empty-eyed woman leaps across the back of her bench, straining to grab the woman and girl.

Hazel shouts a wordless command. She has several days' worth of spells saved in her wand. She does not seek out violence, but it has a way of finding her regardless. Because of this she makes sure she is always prepared.

Every night, whenever she finds herself alone, she uses her magic to fill the wand with power. She says the words, mixes the components, burns the incense, whatever the spell requires. The spell is cast and she catches it, holds it in her mind and hands, and pushes it into the frail, bone white stick where the magic waits for her to release it.

Her wand flashes an ethereal light and the hag's thrall slumps forward, limp and lifeless as a dead snake.

The girl in her arms cries louder. Without looking, she seems to sense the death all around her.

Hazel's wand flashes again and again. Spell after spell escaping and finding targets. Arms straining for her collapse, devoid of life. She is forced to pull the girl with her onto the floor between benches as attackers come from all sides

She ignores the blood pooling around them.

She raises her wand one more time as two figures scramble over the bench toward them. She stops herself from uttering the command as the young boy and girl stare down at her.

Her hand begins to shake and her shoulders heave as she realizes she is crying. She stares up, helpless to do what she knows she must. These children are already gone. She knows that. She just needs to raise the wand, make the soundless command. But they are children. So like a child she still remembers. Like a child she will never see again.

She lowers her wand and wraps Miki in her arms as she

closes her eyes. "I'm so sorry." She says it to every child she has ever failed.

There is a sound. One she recognizes. Blade opening flesh. Gore spilling.

She opens her eyes to find Arthur Shield. His face is expressionless. He doesn't spare a glance for the two small corpses in front of him.

He holds his sword now. Hazel had not noticed him pull it from beneath their bench. Had not thought he would have the time.

But then she realizes that there are no other living things on the cart.

She rises slowly, Miki still held in her arms, her face pressed tightly between her breasts.

"Where's the hag?" she starts to ask. The words are replaced with a scream as the cart crashes.

———

I'd been in a car accident before. It wasn't anything serious. Just a little fender-bender, but it had been terrifying. The sound of crunching plastic and metal, my father cursing, my mother shouting at him to stop.

This was so much worse. It was the first time I learned that horses could scream.

Hazel's screaming was louder, though. She left the ground, still holding me, and began to curse. I couldn't understand the words, but I know swearing when I hear it.

She held me tighter and wrapped her body around me as we flew through the air. From a gap in her protective shell I could see the cart. It almost seemed as though we were floating in place as the cart spun around us.

For an instant I saw Arthur as he flew past my line of

sight. He'd folded himself into a ball, head down and arms held up around his face.

Then my world turned into nothing but the sound of shattering wood and sudden, throbbing pain.

My own sobbing woke me. I found myself lying on my back staring up at the concerned face of Hazel Midd.

She tried to give me a comforting smile, but the fact that the left side of her face was a swollen mess made that hard for her to pull off. She looked up and shouted something.

"Good. Talk to her. Don't let her fall asleep again." Arthur's voice sounded strained and I craned my neck to see him.

Hazel tried to stop me, but I ignored her. I spotted Arthur a short distance off digging through the remains of the cart. It lay on its side in a ditch that ran along the road. The roof of the cart had apparently held all its passenger's luggage. Most of it now lay scattered across the road. Many lay open with various items littered everywhere. We were surrounded by thick trees, leaves still turning red and brown.

Arthur had removed the black vest he'd been wearing and had cut away the bloodstained portion of his sleeves. He seemed oblivious to the cold as he strained to pull a large wooden crate from the wreckage.

"Miki?" I finally realized that Hazel was talking to me.

I looked up at her and blinked. "Yeah?"

"How are you feeling?"

I thought about it and realized I was not doing well. "My leg hurts." I glanced down to find that my right leg was bent in a direction I was pretty sure it wasn't supposed to be.

"I know, sweetie. Arthur's looking for something that should help with that."

I had no idea what was supposed to help with *that*.

As though he could hear her soft tone he shouted at her. "You're sure they're something just anyone would be carrying with them?" I glanced back to find him digging through the trunk.

"Yes. No one travels without them anymore. They opened a bottling plant in East Amethyst." Hazel watched him as she spoke.

He grunted his response and continued to shift the contents of the box.

"What's he doing? Is he stealing those people's stuff?" I asked. Still a little dazed. I felt like I should probably be hurting more, but just wasn't.

"He's just going to borrow something."

Arthur let out a sudden exclamation. "Found one." He strode over and handed Hazel a small glass bottle. "Changed the logo," he commented in a conversational tone.

I studied the small bottle in Hazel's hand. The clear glass container held a red liquid that seemed to give off a slight glow.

"What's that?" I asked, intrigued by the strange fluid.

"A healing potion," Hazel said as she grasped the bottle and twisted with a grunt. There was a popping sound followed by the hissing of released pressure.

"A what?" I asked, confused.

"Would you mind holding her?" Hazel said to Arthur. "This is going to hurt and I don't want her moving before it's done."

He nodded and knelt next to me. I watched, still slightly dazed as he placed a strong hand on either of my shoulders.

Hazel placed the bottle on the ground next to her then

grabbed my leg with soft, cold hands. "This is only going to hurt for a minute, sweetie, okay?"

"What are you—" my question was stopped as Arthur stuck something in my mouth and instructed I bite down.

I stared up at him confused for half a heartbeat. Then Hazel set my broken leg.

I bit down hard on the leather belt before spitting it out and screaming. As my mouth was open Hazel upended the bottle of glowing red liquid into my mouth.

It tasted like cherry. And not that disgusting cough medicine cherry. It tasted like a fresh picked cherry. The potion tickled the back of my throat as it poured into me without even waiting for me to swallow.

The pain of my leg stopped almost instantly.

Arthur lifted his hands from my shoulder and I sat up, wiping away tears that seemed unnecessary now.

"That seemed to work quicker than I remember," he said to Hazel.

She nodded. "Big money in potions these days. Lots of alchemists trying to one-up each other."

He grunted as though all those nonsense words made sense to him.

"Was that medicine?" I asked them.

"Yes. Do you feel better?" Arthur asked me.

I considered a little before nodding. My head was suddenly clear of the fog it had been under before. I noticed that my blood-soaked winter coat had been laid under my leg to keep it elevated. I remembered that was important to do, for some reason.

"I'm cold." I looked from Arthur to Hazel.

Arthur rose and approached one of the many bags that lay on the ground. He opened one seemingly at random and pulled something out. He returned and indicated I stand up.

I did so, and with no ceremony he lay the cloak over my shoulders, clasping it across my chest, and pulled the hood up.

"Better?" he asked.

I nodded, admiring the deep green fabric. It was so soft.

"Are you sure that's okay?" Hazel asked.

"Think they're going to want it back?" His tone was suddenly cold.

Hazel shrunk back slightly but shook her head. "You're right."

"You should take what you need as well. But be quick. The hag is likely still close."

I watched as the two of them each emptied bags onto the road and began to fill it with various items from the other bags.

Arthur returned carrying two bags. He handed me the smaller of the two. "Can you carry that?" he asked.

"What's this for?" I asked.

"Clothes for you."

"Oh." I slung the bag over my shoulder the way he and Hazel had done theirs. I felt weird about having a bag full of clothes just picked up on the side of the road, but I'd been taught to be grateful when anyone gives you something. "Thanks."

"Come on." Arthur held out a hand.

Reluctantly, I reached up and took it. His thick fingers completely enveloped my hand as he led us away from the cart.

Hazel took up position on my other side, and without thinking, I grasped her hand as well. She gave me a weak smile before returning her attention to the trees that surrounded us.

I glanced back toward the cart one final time. From out of a broken window I noticed for the first time the body of the dead man. He lay draped, half-in-half-out of the vehicle.

I looked away quickly and tried very hard not to start crying again.

AMETHYST LAKE

IT DIDN'T TAKE LONG before I completely forgot I'd even broken my leg. All I could think about was how much I hated all this walking.

Eventually, just to shut me up, Arthur picked me up and sat me on his shoulders. I hummed contentedly as Arthur and Hazel had a hushed conversation in the language Hazel had called Imperial.

Arthur seemed to be asking her something, but she kept just shaking her head.

"Whatcha guys talking 'bout?" I asked, finally. Despite everything I suddenly felt better than I had in at least the last two days. That meant I wanted to talk. I liked talking to people. Hazel was nice, so I liked talking to her. And even though he seemed grumpy most of the time, Arthur had been kind to me. So, talking to him seemed acceptable.

"It's nothing, sweetie." Hazel was lying. I knew that. I'd always been able to tell when mom was lying to me. Hazel intoned her voice with the same syrupy sweetness mom had whenever she didn't want to tell me something.

"Mikaia?" Arthur asked, surprising me with the use of

my full name instead of the shortened version everyone usually used.

"Yeah?" I asked, leaning forward in my seat to peer down at his face.

"You'd like to be able to talk to people, right? People other than just Hazel and I?"

"Sure!" I answered, suddenly excited by that prospect.

Arthur didn't reply, just nodded and glanced at Hazel who was shaking her head and mumbling something under her breath.

"Well?" Arthur said, finally. "Will you do it?"

"Fine." Hazel glared at him. "Once we get to town, I'll see if I can find all the ingredients."

"Thank you." While he didn't sound smug, I still got the feeling that he'd just won some sort of argument and was pleased with himself.

Hazel sighed and returned her attention to the road.

The rest of the trip was one of the most boring I'd ever been forced to take. The most exciting moment was the sudden appearance of a herd of deer crossing the road from a thick copse of trees.

Arthur stopped to allow me the chance to point and marvel at the creatures, then he resumed walking.

We stopped for a few bathroom breaks, and he insisted on sending Hazel with me into the trees, despite my own insistence that I knew what I was doing.

Eventually the town of Amethyst Lake came into view. We rounded a corner on the road and suddenly there were no more trees.

This town was much larger than the last one. In fact, it could only be called a city. A stone wall surrounded it, with stone and brick buildings rising from behind. Beside the walled city rested a large lake. Crystallin blue water stretched for miles away from the walls.

I pointed out several boats out on the surface and Hazel told me they were fishermen. "They'll all be coming in before the sun sets," she told me. "We'll have to make sure you see the lake when the sun sets, Miki. It's so beautiful."

Arthur stopped us a short distance before the gate. A fat man in leather armor watched us from a seat on a box against the wall. "Here." Arthur pulled a small pouch from his bag. "You know this city, right?"

"I do," Hazel said, accepting the pouch from Arthur. It clinked as she did so.

"What'd be your first choice of inn?" he asked her.

She thought before answering. "Probably the Silver Hare."

He nodded. "Perfect. Get a room for you and Mikaia there. I'll be along later. I'm going to go and let the local guards know about the cart."

"Are you going to tell them what happened?" Hazel asked.

He nodded. "They should definitely know that there's a hag in their woods. After you have the room, you have some shopping to do."

Hazel scowled at that. "I know."

Arthur lifted me off his shoulders and placed me on the ground next to Hazel. "Listen to Hazel, all right?"

I nodded my understanding and, unbidden, grabbed the woman's hand.

"Good. I'll see the two of you tonight."

Arthur strode ahead of us and waved to the guard as he got closer. The man clumsily rose and approached the older man.

I couldn't hear what they said, but the man's expression

grew grim as Arthur spoke to him. He spared us a glance as we passed, giving Hazel a nod of acknowledgement, before turning back to his conversation with Arthur.

We passed through the gates and were in the city of Amethyst Lake.

I was able to hold in my awe for a whole two seconds. The city was amazing! The stone buildings looked just like something out of a movie. And the *people*! Many of the women wore the same simple style of dress as Hazel, but there were almost just as many dressed in bright, colorful fabric. Men in hooded cloaks or polished armor. Others wore shirts of different colorful patterns.

And, the part that excited me the most, there were so many who weren't human. Back home I'd known people of other races. I had many goblin "cousins" and a few gnome friends at school. But the whole city of Summervale only had one dwarf and one elf. Here there were clumps of every race. I saw a dwarf buying fruit from a gnome, an elf laughing with a human. There was a woman with bright red skin and a long, supple tail. Short horns poked out from her dark hair. I stared in open awe at her. Then I saw the orc.

I tugged at Hazel's sleeve. "I thought Arthur said orcs weren't popular around here?"

She nodded. "Doesn't mean they're not allowed. Just that they have to be careful."

"Oh." We walked on for a while as I watched the orc man passing us. "Careful with what?" I asked again.

"Just to stay out of trouble."

"Like with the police?" I asked.

Hazel nodded. "Exactly."

"It's the same back home. But my Uncle Jack helps get us out of trouble any time any of my other uncles get caught."

She looked down at me. "Really? How does he do that?"

"He's friends with Detective Denny."

Hazel furrowed her brow. "What's a detective?"

I opened my mouth but realized I didn't know how to answer. "Well, Detective Denny is an elf. She likes Uncle Jack and likes to help him. She says I'm not supposed to tell him that, though. Cause the 'dumb bastard' would get the wrong idea."

"Language," she warned, though she said it with a smile.

We went a little deeper into the city, Hazel patiently answering any questions I came up with. Finally, she stopped us in front of a whitewashed stone building. Above the door was a plaque with a picture of a silver rabbit running across its surface.

"Here we are."

Inside was a small white room with a desk and a gnome woman seated behind it.

She looked up at us and offered a friendly smile. She said something in Imperial and Hazel replied by reaching into the leather pouch Arthur had given her. She placed two silver coins on the counter.

The gnome smiled wider and handed Hazel a key after writing something in a large ledger.

"Alright, come on, sweetie." Hazel grabbed my hand again and led me up a flight of stairs the gnome had indicated.

———

Arthur stands with the group of guards around the remains of the cart. Inside the cart two men with lanterns investigate the carnage.

One man pokes his head out through a broken window. "How many passengers you say there was?"

"At least ten beside myself and my companions."

"The pretty lady and the little girl?" The fat guard asks. He'd noted them at the city's gate.

Arthur nods.

"What's the story there?" he grins, lopsided. "You seem awful long in the beard for a pretty little thing like that."

"She's the child's caretaker."

"Kid yours?" the man presses.

Arthur shakes his head.

"Right. Cause you're a paladin of Saban, right? No kids for you."

"That's actually a misconception," Arthur points out. "There are no rules against that in the order."

"Really?" another of the guards asks. "I'd heard you were all, you know..."

The guard in the cart interrupts. "I'm only seeing four bodies in here. You sure you counted ten?"

Arthur feels the old familiar chill. He glances around the woods, hand resting on his sword hilt.

"What is it?" the fat one asks again.

"I told you there was a hag in the cart."

The guards exchange looks. "Yeah, you did." The captain orders the wagon they'd brought along closer. "Let's load up the bodies. See about getting them to a priest before burying them."

"Can't he do that?" another guard says, nodding toward Arthur.

The captain hesitates. "Can you?"

"What? Offer last rights?" Arthur shakes his head. "No. I was never a priest."

"There you go," the captain says to the other man.

"Now load them up. Regardless of rights, we can't just leave 'em out here."

The group makes quick work of the remaining bodies. Arthur notes, as they cover them with the thick canvas in the cart, that these four were those that Hazel Midd had dealt with using her wand. The bodies he had dealt with have gone.

There had been one corpse dangling from the window. A trail of dried blood covered the wood beside that. It could have poured from an open wound, or it could have been smeared there as the man crawled out of the cart.

Despite the feeling of impending danger, a feeling that has never betrayed him, nothing happens. The bodies are loaded, and they leave the wreckage without incident.

He feels her eyes on him, though. He knows it's her. From the shadows in the wood, Grannie Summer watches him.

From the back of the horse the guards have given him he feels the icy touch of her magic. He refuses to show her that he is disturbed by this.

"You care not for the child?" the voice asks. "Then why protect her? Why not just let me have her?"

He shakes his head, trying to force her from his mind.

"I see. A promise made. A promise to... an enemy? Why hold to these promises, Knight of Saban?"

He feels her pressing deeper into his mind. How is she doing this?

"Oh." The fingers dig into his memories and stop. They stop half a year ago. The night Saban died.

The forest suddenly echoes with the sound of laughter. The horses pick up their pace, unbidden. The men glance around, hands on weapons. Arthur urges his horse to run. It complies willingly. The others follow. The cart rattles and jolts, its morbid cargo bouncing with the unsafe speed. The cackling laughter follows them all the way back to the walls of the city.

———

We left our things in our room and Hazel took me back out into the city. She asked around for a shop to find ingredients. When I asked what the ingredients were for she pretended to not hear my question.

Finally, we entered a dimly lit shop. A wizened old woman behind the counter looked up and smiled at us. "Welcome, welcome. What can I do for you?"

"Hazel's looking for ingredients," I answered.

Hazel looked down at me. "You can understand her?" she asked.

I nodded.

Hazel approached the woman behind her counter. "I need all the ingredients for a comprehension spell."

"A what?" the old woman asked, nervous eyes glancing around the empty room.

"We're not speaking Imperial. So, if nothing else, you know about the spell."

The woman's eyes opened wide in sudden understanding. "Ah. I see. Who is the spell for?"

Hazel looked down at me.

I frowned and jabbed a finger into my chest. "Me?"

"She doesn't speak Imperial and her..." she paused, seemingly unhappy with what she had to say, "her guardian wants her to be able to understand everybody."

"That is a cruel spell to cast on a child." The old woman gave me a weighted look. "You're sure?"

Hazel nodded. "I argued against it, but he's convinced it's for the best."

"Did he... convince you?" The woman waved a hand over the side of her face, indicating the mass of bruising on Hazel's cheek.

"No," Hazel answered. "But if you have something that might help get the swelling down, I would appreciate it."

"All right then. Wait right there." The old woman struggled to her feet and disappeared behind a curtain of fabric strands braided with beads.

Hazel tapped a foot impatiently as the old woman hummed to herself behind the curtain. She returned a few minutes later with an armful of dried plants and bottles of cloudy liquid.

"You know the spell, I assume?" she asked Hazel.

"I do."

"So you know the ingredient I can't sell you?"

Hazel sighed. "Yes, yes, I know."

"Okay. Well, that will be five gold imperials."

"What?" Hazel let out a choked cry.

"It's ten silver for the ingredients and four and nine gold for my silence."

"Your silence?"

"That's right. We're so close to Glanzend here. Who knows when one of Saban's dogs could show up."

Hazel let out another choked breath, but she placed five gold coins on the counter. "That's dirty, you old crone."

The woman shrugged. "It's business, my girl. Just business."

Hazel swept the ingredients off the counter and into her bag. She glared at the old woman as she grabbed my hand and led me back outside.

"Please come again!" the woman cackled as we shut the door behind us.

"Filthy old crone," Hazel muttered to herself as she led us back to the Silver Hare.

I recognized that she was angry about something, so I kept my questions to myself until we were back in our room.

"What did you mean by spell?" I asked as Hazel dumped the contents of her bag out on the room's single bed.

"Arthur asked me to cast a spell on you." She avoided looking at me while she organized the bottles and plants.

"Really?" I excitedly jumped up on the bed so I was eye level with her.

"Yes, now stop bouncing like that. You might damage the dried mandrake."

I stopped bouncing and sat down to watch as she produced a stone bowl from somewhere under her robe. She muttered to herself in a language I couldn't understand as she broke off pieces from the dried bundles and began to crush them in the bowl.

She popped the cork on one of the bottles and sniffed it. Her nose wrinkled in distaste but she poured a few drops into the bowl.

"Okay," she said, finally. "That just leaves the last ingredient."

"What's that?" I asked.

"Do you really want to be able to talk to everybody, Miki?" she asked me.

I nodded. "Yeah."

"Okay. Well, this spell will make it so you can talk to anybody you meet. You'll understand them and they'll understand you."

"Cool." I stared at the bowl of paste she'd made. A rank odor drifted up from it.

"There's just one thing I'm going to need."

"What?" I asked.

"A drop of your blood."

"Oh, that's easy. Mom took me to get my blood tested once. Here." I held out my arm toward her. I closed my eyes tightly and looked away. "Do it quick before I get scared."

"Sorry, sweetie, not like that."

I opened my eyes and looked up at her. She looked so sad. From somewhere she'd produced a long, slender needle.

"Then how?" I asked, growing more nervous.

"I'm going to need you to stick out your tongue for me."

"Like dis?" I stuck my tongue out and laughed a little.

The needle biting into my tongue hurt more than the cart crash had. That's how it felt anyway. It was probably just the betrayal.

I cried through the rest of the spell. The pain had stopped long ago but I couldn't get over the fact that Hazel, someone I had *trusted*, had just shoved a needle into my tongue.

It was worse the second time. Without even asking if I was okay, she smeared the needle with the paste, now including some of my tongue blood, and jammed it into my arm.

I yanked my arm away, pulling the needle out of her hand and ran to the other side of the room. I pulled the needle out of my forearm and threw it back across the room toward Hazel. "That hurt!" I declared.

"I know, sweetie." She crossed the room and tried to pull me into a hug.

I batted her away with a pair of angry, flailing fists. She ignored them and scooped me up.

"It's done now, Miki. It's done."

I sniffed loudly and glared up at her. "You promise?"

"I promise. Can I make it up to you?"

I thought about that. "Do you know any songs?"

"Songs?" She gave me a confused look.

"Back home, whenever I felt sick Uncle Jack would come visit and sing to me. I always felt better after that."

"What song would he sing for you?" she asked.

"The ants go marching," I answered through another sniffle.

"I don't know that one. Do you want to sing it for me?"

I considered that for a moment. I'd never had to sing the song before. Maybe it would still work? "Okay."

Hazel laid me down on the bed and curled up next to me. She put her head on the pillow and waited while I tried to remember the words.

———

After singing to Hazel I couldn't bring myself to stay mad at her.

I let her wash my face using the small basin in the room and then let her lead me back downstairs.

This inn also had a little tavern attached to the first floor. Hazel led us in there and using some of the coins from the bag Arthur had given her she bought us food.

She got herself a small mug of something that smelled like my grandmother would have liked it and a cup of something sweet and fizzy for me. I couldn't quite place the flavor, but I liked it.

The food was simple enough, though it felt like a step up from the meat and bread from the previous day.

As I scooped a heaping spoonful of stew into my mouth I realized that I hadn't actually eaten anything in almost a full day.

I'd finished my bowl before Hazel had even started on hers. She looked up from her own spoon to find me staring at her bowl with hungry eyes.

She grinned and slid the bowl over to me. "Eat up, sweetie."

I grinned back and did as she asked.

She waved down a short woman—I realized she was a dwarf much later—and ordered a second bowl for herself.

"Right away, Miss," the waitress replied and hurried off.

"I understood her," I said through a mouthful of stew.

Hazel nodded. "You should be able to understand anyone now." She didn't seem as happy about that as I did.

"What's wrong?" I asked between spoonfuls.

Hazel shook her head. "I just hope Arthur knows what he's doing. Taking you to Glanzend after having me cast that spell on you. Not to mention your..." she trailed off.

"My what?"

She shook her head. "They don't really like orcs where we're going, sweetie."

"I know. You told me that already." I shrugged. I was used to people being stupid about that. It hurt more than I'd ever have admitted, but I was good at hiding that pain.

"It's good that you look human." Hazel studied me.

I furrowed my brow a little at that. I was half-human, sure, but pretending like one half of my heritage was something I should be ashamed of left me angry.

"I don't mean it like that, hon." Hazel reached across the

table and put a hand on mine. I was gripping my spoon so hard it was shaking. "I just mean it will be safer for you."

I nodded. I still didn't know why it should matter, but I also knew that it did. People were always going to hate others for being different.

That was why my grandmother had been killed, after all. The memory of her absence suddenly welled up inside me. It had only been six months since she'd been murdered. But I was young and able to move on quicker than I really would have liked.

My father hadn't told me much about her death, only that she had been killed by a man who hated orcs and had held a grudge against her in particular.

"But he's gone now, Mik. You never have to worry about that. Your mother and I and your Uncle Jack, we're always going to be here to protect you from people like him."

That's what he'd said. But now? Now, he and mom and Jack were nowhere to be seen. All I had was Hazel, a woman who had less than an hour ago stabbed me *twice* with a needle just because my other protector, an old man who barely spoke to me, had told her to.

Hazel seemed to sense my mood and pulled her hand back. She watched me eat in silence for a while. When her new bowl arrived she ate a few spoonfuls before offering it to me.

I shook my head and stared at the few globs of stew clinging to my bowl.

Hazel took a few more bites of her food before pushing herself up. "Sun should be setting soon. Do you want to go and see the lake?"

I considered for a moment before nodding my head solemnly.

"Okay. Come on." Hazel held out a hand and I took it.

The magic the city had once held was lost to me. The thoughts of my family, which I had somehow avoided for so long, pressed down on me.

The mood lifted slightly when Hazel began to lead me up a flight of stairs.

"Where are we going?" I asked.

"To the top of the city wall. They let people up on this side because it just faces the lake. And the view is so nice that everybody wants to see it."

Once we reached the top of the stairs I saw that she was right. There was a crowd of people on the wide walkway that was the top of the city walls. Parents with children on their shoulders or held tightly by their hands, loving couples pressed close, as well as more than a few lonely people trying to ignore everyone else.

We approached a stone battlement that rose higher than my head, and Hazel lifted me up and set me on the cold stone.

I let out an excited noise at the site of the lake stretching out below the city. As far as I could see in front of me was crystal clear water. Boats moved back and forth along its surface. Turning toward the direction of the gates we entered when we first arrived I could see the shore as it wrapped around. In the other direction, the lake, again, seemed to stretch beyond the horizon.

"How far does it go?" I asked, looking over my shoulder at Hazel.

She thought about it. "I'm not actually sure. Far, though."

"What's on the other side?"

She smiled. "On the other side of the lake there's actually a very famous school."

I frowned. Why would anyone be that excited about a school.

"They train wizards there. And they have the biggest library in the world."

"Wizards?" I perked up at that. "I thought magic was bad?"

She laughed softly as she rested her arms on the wall next to me. "Magic can't be bad. Just what some people do with it. But it's not that magic is bad, it's just that some people don't like all kinds of magic. That school teaches the magic that most people like."

"What kind of magic?" I asked, excited.

She shrugged. "I don't know. Lots." She thought some. "You remember that drink we gave you earlier that fixed your leg?"

I nodded.

"They teach their students how to make potions like that. Stuff that can help people. Or make people rich." She added that last part with a touch of scorn.

"I want to be a wizard," I said, turning back to the lake and straining to see across the water. As much as I tried I couldn't see this magic school.

Hazel ruffled my hair fondly. "I'm sure you'd make a great wizard, Miki."

"I know." I grinned up at her, my depression from moments before forgotten.

"Oh, look." Hazel pointed out toward the water. "Sun's setting."

I turned to find that the sun had sunk lower when I wasn't watching. I realized now, after spending at least two days in this world, that the sun didn't look right. Not like the one I was used to anyway. It was a little redder, slightly larger in the sky. But I didn't dwell on it. As the bottom of the glowing circle passed beneath the water-lined horizon the water changed. The crystal surface was still clear and clean, but it changed from a crystalline blue to a magnificent purple hue.

"That's why it's called Amethyst Lake," Hazel whispered to me as the other spectators around us reacted to the sight.

"I love it," I said.

We watched until the sun had set completely. Until the water turned black and the lights of the city behind us cast the wall's shadow over its surface. We only left when all the others—except a few distracted couples—had left as well.

I fell asleep before we made it back to the inn. I woke in the room's single bed. Next to me Hazel snored softly.

I snuggled closer to her and, with the help of her steady snoring, fell back asleep.

———

Arthur is almost disappointed when the young gnome behind the Silver Hare's front desk confirms that a young woman and girl have a room there.

Part of him—more than he will admit to himself—still hopes that the young witch will just take the orc girl and run away from him. He knows she wants to. Can see the thought play behind her eyes every time she looks at him.

But she doesn't. She got a room at the inn like she said she would and hasn't fled in the night. Which means that Arthur is still responsible for the girl.

A girl that, less than a year ago, he had planned on killing.

That was before his god died, though. Before he was forced to face a reality that he never thought he would.

Gods die. And if they die, are they truly gods? Is their will truly divine?

He does not regret killing the girl's grandmother. That orc woman had been a criminal. A worthy opponent, true, but a criminal. He *does* now regret some of the others he's killed.

After the death of Saban, Arthur had spent too many nights wondering just how much of the blood on his hands had been that of innocents.

He forces these thoughts from his mind and pays the gnome for a room. He knows he should probably feel guilty for using money stolen from the dead, but he doesn't. That was another idea put in his head by a god that might have only been a man. And Arthur has always had a tendency for the pragmatic.

What good would have leaving the coins done? None. What god would punish him for taking it? None. The god of justice was dead, after all.

He takes a room on the bottom floor. The cheapest they have. The gnome tries to convince him that for only a few copper coins more he could have a much more comfortable bed. He declines. He does not think he could sleep on anything more comfortable and tells her so.

He signs his name in a ledger and accepts the key given him.

He allows himself the vain hope that Hazel Midd, the witch, will take the girl in the night. That as he sleeps, she will just slip away.

But he knows this won't happen. For whatever reason, the witch wants to go to Glanzend. Has business there. She is a smart woman, Arthur concedes. She obviously knows that her purpose will be easier to accomplish with him at her side.

Lying on his bed—it is still too soft for him to sleep comfortably—he idly wonders if he should turn her over to the authorities. She is a witch, after all. The type of magic she practices is illegal in the empire. Though, that law is only truly enforced in Glanzend itself. Only where the paladins of Saban are powerful enough to do so.

He wonders, however, if that is still the case. It has been over twenty years since he'd left this world. Six months since the death of Saban. The paladins would have no power left. Nothing that wasn't granted them by the empire, anyway.

Regardless of the order's power, though, he is sure that a witch will not be welcome in Glanzend.

He decides against it. Since he's allowed himself the right to question the beliefs he's always held he has met people, made friends with more than a few users of magic that many would consider evil or dark. He trusted those individuals with his life, and they had trusted him. He hopes they are well.

He thinks of a young witch, barely past her sixteenth year. Nothing at all like Hazel Midd, but close enough that he feels guilt at even considering handing her over to the order's witch hunters.

He would not lie about it if asked, but he would not be the one to reveal her true nature.

But what of the girl? He will have to remind her to lie about her name. The name Goretusk still seemed to hold power in the land, based on the reactions of those villagers he'd protected her from. The hatred that had come from that elf woman at the mere sight of an orc child. It reminded him of himself not so long ago. It makes him sick to remember.

How could he ever have considered murdering that

child? She seems to trust him explicitly. How could he possibly have earned that trust?

It doesn't matter. He made a promise to protect her. In the absence of his faith all he has left is his pride and the scrap of honor that his life has allowed him to keep.

He rolls onto his side and stares at a dark shadow on the wall and prays to an empty heaven to be saved from himself.

———

The sound of a heavy fist against our door woke me the next morning.

I sat up in bed and glanced down at Hazel who seemed oblivious to the knocking. A rivulet of saliva travelled down her face and pooled on the pillow, mixing with the thick cream she'd applied the night before to her bruised and swollen face.

I thought about shaking her awake but instead untangled her arms from around my waist and slid off the soft bed.

The floor of the room was cold, and I could feel it even through the thin rug.

I stood on my tiptoes and unlocked the door and swung it open.

Arthur stared down at me.

"Morning," I mumbled as I looked up at him.

For a second I thought I saw disappointment in his eyes, but it passed. "Where's Hazel?" he asked.

I turned and pointed toward the bed where the woman was still snoring.

Arthur remained in the doorway. "Wake her up. Both of you get dressed and meet me at the front entrance. Okay?"

I nodded before turning toward the bed.

"No going back to sleep," he said before closing the door.

I did seriously consider climbing back under the warm blankets of the bed, but I did what Arthur had asked.

Hazel woke with a snort and sat upright when I shook her leg.

"Wazit?" she looked around with glazed over eyes.

"Arthur says to get ready and meet him outside," I said through a yawn.

"Oh." She blinked a few times as she tried to focus on me. "G'morning."

"Good morning."

"What'd you say?"

I repeated myself and she climbed out of bed.

Hazel helped me get dressed in the new clothes Arthur had found for me before the two of us made our way to the floor's communal facilities.

I tried to ignore all the other women going about their morning routines as I sat on the polished wood of the toilet seat. Hazel was thoughtful enough to stand in the opening of the stall where there should have been a door.

Once I'd relieved myself and allowed Hazel to wash my hands and face with the strange bathroom's basin, the two of us made our way outside.

Arthur sitting on a stone planter in front of the building, a tapping foot the only sign of his impatience.

"Ready to go?" He asked.

Hazel nodded. Both looked at me and waited until I did the same.

"Good. It should only be another day or so by carriage to Glanzend. I've already bought our tickets. It leaves in fifteen minutes."

"What?" Hazel asked as she pulled me after Arthur,

who had already turned and started down the street. "Why so soon?"

"I thought you'd be quicker to wake up and get ready. Hurry up. I was told refunds aren't an option."

I was dragged through the streets as Hazel tried to keep up with the old man who, despite his age, walked with a long stride that ate the cobble streets.

I managed to ask about breakfast once before Hazel asked me to be quiet. I didn't appreciate being silenced but I decided it was best to just do as she asked. My stomach was aching for food, though, and I made a mental note to complain as soon as we were done walking.

We were the last ones on the carriage. It was almost an exact clone of the last one. I felt a slight pang of anxiety as I climbed the steps inside.

The driver, sitting on a bench on the roof, tipped a tall blue hat at Hazel and I as we entered. I returned the hat tip with a wave. The man's friendly smile almost helped with the fear.

Once inside the cart Hazel glanced around to find Arthur waving us over to the bench in the very back. It was the only one open. We made our way to the back, trying to avoid hitting anyone with the bags on our backs or tripping over the bags the other passengers had left half in the aisle.

Arthur slid over to one end of the bench and indicated we should sit in the open area. Hazel picked me up and put me in the corner by the window and sat herself next to Arthur.

"So, what happens when we get to Glanzend?" she whispered.

He shrugged. "I'll go to the temple. You can do whatever you need to. I'd appreciate it if you stayed with the girl, though."

Hazel nodded as though that were obvious. "Of course. I wouldn't let you just *take* her to those..." she stopped. "I'm sorry."

Arthur just shrugged and looked out his window. "It's fine."

The cart jolted and began to move. I stood in my seat and stared out the window. I watched as the cart drove out of the carriage house. I waved at people waiting for their rides, at drivers, and their horses. Some waved back, but most just stared ahead, seemingly bored with the whole affair.

The cart drove through town and then out a gate, almost identical to the one we'd entered, but I knew it was on the other side of town. The road here was wider, and the trees sparser. I was excited to see that the lake was perfectly visible. I watched the boats flit across its surface.

I was glad I was awake this time. I must have missed so much while I slept in the last cart.

At some point I did fall asleep again. I woke occasionally and glanced back out the window before sitting back down and putting my head back in Hazel's lap.

I forgot to complain about the lack of breakfast.

GLANZEND

He occasionally glances down to watch the girl sleep. She snores softly, mouth open wide to reveal the two small tusks that betray her heritage.

The hatred he has harbored for her kind twists in his belly again and he forces his trembling hand to still. The closer to the capital they get, the stronger his old feelings of animosity seem to grow.

But the child is innocent. He knows that now. One of the first truths he forced himself to acknowledge after Saban's death was that a parent's sins should not be transferred to the child.

Burning a field, root and branch, was not the just thing to do.

"You feeling alright?" Hazel asks him.

Her question surprises him so he answers honestly. "I am not looking forward to seeing the temple again."

He glances down to find her expression confused. "Why not? I thought all you paladins loved that eyesore?"

He raises an eyebrow. "Eyesore? I thought that

regardless of religious leaning that the temple compound is quite beautiful."

She shrugs. "I guess. I just can't separate what's done inside with it. Honestly, I've never even seen it. Just pictures."

"What do you mean by, what's done inside?" he asks.

She rolls her eyes at him. "Oh, come on. How long have you been a member of that cult?"

He grinds his teeth but remains silent. She seems to realize what she has said and cringes. "I'm sorry. I keep forgetting myself."

"I was a member of Saban's order for twenty years before I left. I was faithful for nearly twenty years in my absence. I know of nothing untoward being done behind those walls. Now tell me what you meant."

"Twenty years, huh? Long time to be away from home." She strokes Mikaia's hair as she speaks, voice sad.

"It is."

"So, you wouldn't know."

"Know what?"

"About ten years ago things changed. No one knows why. The paladins just got, I dunno, stricter? I guess that's the politest word I can use."

"Stricter?" The thought almost makes him laugh. The order of Saban has always held that the law should be followed to the letter. Nothing could be stricter than that.

She nods. "Yeah. Saban's prophet started making decrees. Convinced the Empress to write them into law. Harsh laws." She does not look at him as she speaks. Just studies the sleeping girl with a look of sadness remembered.

"Prophet?" Arthur asks. The order never had a prophet. Why would it need one with Saban present? The god sat on his throne and made his own decrees. Those had always been the same: obey the law and uphold peace.

She looks up, confused again. "Yeah. I thought you were one of his paladins? Why wouldn't you know about the prophet?"

Arthur's mind, quicker than many give him credit for, turns. It is easier for him to accept new ideas than even he could have known, and he has always had an uncanny ability for connecting unfamiliar ideas and seeing the whole picture. The thought enters his mind and he suddenly knows that it must be true.

"What year is it, Hazel?" he asks.

"Eight Hundred Four." He had not thought it possible for her to look more confused.

He sighs deeply and rests his head against the back wall of the cart. "I see." He has not been gone for twenty years. He has been gone for thirty.

Time must not run at the same speed between these two worlds. Or something happened when he and the girl were pulled into the tear between.

"What is it?" she asks him.

"Nothing, really. I just realized that I might not have as many friends left in the temple as I thought."

Hazel sits in silence for a time, still compulsively smoothing out the young girl's messy hair. The blond nest really could use a brush. He will have to buy her one in Glanzend.

He stops to consider that thought. Why would he think that? Why should he care if the child is presentable? His only goal is to find a wizard powerful enough to open a doorway to send her home. Not to keep her comfortable and happy.

"When we get to the city, you should take Mikaia. Find a good inn. Maybe get her a bath."

Hazel looks up at his words. "Yeah?"

"Yes. Take care of her. Make sure she's comfortable. I'll go to the temple alone and see about ensuring her safety first. Then I'll help you with whatever errand it was you have in the capital."

Hazel hesitates, then speaks. "My errand is actually in the temple."

This surprises him, but he realizes it shouldn't. Why else would she be willing to attach herself to a man she obviously hates. He nods. "That's why you never just took the girl and ran, isn't it?"

"I thought about it," she admits. "But if you are who you say, then you can help me."

"What makes you so sure I will help you?"

She smiles sadly. "I'm not. I just... I trust you for some reason."

That hurts him. He wishes people wouldn't trust him. Saban had trusted him. Saban had trusted Arthur Shield from the first time the young man had stepped onto the training ground inside the temple. That trust had gotten the god killed.

Killed by an orc in a cheap suit.

But she does trust him. Despite only knowing him for two days and despite a contradictory hatred, she trusts him. Along with the pain this trust brings, it also brings a small swell of pride.

"I will help you. You have my word," he says it before he can stop himself. But the promise is made now. And he has already convinced himself that even if he has nothing else he can still keep his word.

She nods, accepting his word as though she had

expected it all along. He hopes he does not regret all these promises he has made.

———

I woke up as Hazel lifted me from my seat. I didn't say anything, though. I was afraid if she knew I was awake she would put me down and make me walk.

As insurance I used a little trick I knew always worked on adults and wrapped my arms around her neck and let out a tired, but contented sigh.

Hazel's grip tightened for an instant before she let go with one arm to pick up my bag from the bench.

We were at the back of the cart, so there was no one behind us as Hazel carried me to the front. Just Arthur. He noticed me as I watched him and gave a stoic nod.

I forgot about my act and raised a hand to wave at him.

He let out a sigh and half-raised a finger on one hand in response.

I accepted that I probably couldn't expect more from the old man.

"Finally awake?" Hazel asked as she carried me down the steps of the cart.

I knew I'd been found out so I just nodded into her shoulder.

"Get a good rest?"

Another nod.

"Good." She didn't put me down and I allowed myself a small smile to celebrate.

Outside the cart I was hit with the noise of the city. It had been there before, but it had been dulled a little by the walls of the cart. Now I had nothing to protect me from its full force.

Hazel had told me that Glanzend was the biggest city in the empire, and at that moment I was sure that every one of its residents was speaking at once.

It reminded me of a trip my family took once to New York. All that was missing was the sound of the cars, with their honking horns and screeching tires. That was replaced with the whinny of horses and the clatter of wooden wheels on cobblestone.

But, worse than the sound, there was the *smell*. Thick and cloying. It was the scent of too many bodies close together along with a strange mix of industrial smoke and manure.

Arthur seemed unfazed by the sounds and smells, as well as the throng of people that we were attempting to push our way through.

Hazel didn't have the old man's gifts for crowds, though, and tightened her grip on me as she tried to maneuver through the mass of bodies.

Arthur noticed the problem and pushed his way in front of us. The crowd seemed to part, as though by magic, whenever exposed to his blank stare.

I did my best to study our surroundings as we went. We were in a large courtyard surrounded by tall stone walls. There were more people climbing out of carts just like the one we'd just left.

A low wall divided the courtyard in two. Our side was filled with people disembarking, while the other had a steady stream of people entering the courtyard from a large door. This crowd, just as large as ours, was flowing toward a line of waiting carts. People were presenting tickets and climbing up into the vehicles.

I marveled that any one place could have this many people coming and going at the same time.

No one ever really came to my hometown, and it was almost unheard of for anyone to leave.

There had been some cousins, or aunts and uncles, that left, but they almost always came back. Summervale was just their home, they always said. Best place for orcs in the world.

I didn't see any orcs in the crowd. It was almost exclusively human. Every now and then a dwarf would pop up. I guessed there might be a gnome or two somewhere in the throng, but if there was, they were likely hidden by their towering neighbors.

I turned in Hazel's grip and she let out a soft cry at my sudden movement. Luckily, she didn't drop me.

From my vantage point in Hazel's arms, I could see over Arthur's shoulder toward our destination.

There was a large opening in one of the walls that surrounded the courtyard. Along the width of the opening was a row of five wooden turnstiles. Each of those had a guard dressed in armor overseeing the flow of people exiting.

Occasionally one of them would hold up a hand and stop the line. Every time this happened there was an audible groan from the line that had formed behind the person being stopped. Some people attempted to flow over into a neighboring line, but most waited impatiently as the guards inspected a pile of paper handed to them by the traveler they'd stopped. Once satisfied with whatever was on the paper they allowed the line to move again.

I watched the whole process with interest as we slowly moved closer. The closer we got to the opening, the more of the city I was able to see on the other side of the wall. Not enough to form a solid image of the place, but I could see carts and people moving past. There was something that looked like a street vendor's booth. There were boxes of fruit all around it and a gnome woman was holding out trays of sliced fruit to everyone that walked past. No one seemed to pay her any mind.

The closer we got the more excited I was to actually see what waited on the other side. I had gotten so excited that I was squirming in Hazel's arms without realizing it.

"Calm down, sweetie," Hazel said, voice as patient as ever.

I tried to stop, forcing myself to focus even harder on the gnome woman and the street around her.

Then, we were there. Arthur stepped up and placed a hand on the wood of the turnstile.

The armored guard sidestepped in front of the gate and placed his own hand on the gate, stopping Arthur from pushing it open. "Papers, sir." His tone was bored. He obviously did this a lot and was beyond actually caring who he stopped.

Arthur opened his mouth to say something when Hazel stepped around him. Still carrying me, she dug around in her robe and pulled out a small booklet. "Here you go, sir." She shoved the paper into the man's hand before he could respond.

"I didn't ask for your papers, ma'am. I asked for his." He still opened the book and flipped through the pages.

"He's with me." Her voice trembled only slightly as she adjusted her grip on me.

The guard's eyes flicked up from the book to study Hazel, me, and Arthur. "Business in the city?"

"Personal," Arthur answered.

The guard seemed to take note of him again. Actually looking at him he stood up a little straighter. "You look familiar. We met before?"

Arthur shook his head. "I haven't been in Glanzend in almost thirty years."

The man's eyes widened slightly before he shakes his head and laughs to himself. "Sorry. I just realized. You look just like the old statue outside Saban's Temple. You ever do any modeling?"

"Statue?" Arthur asked.

"Guess you wouldn't have seen it. Thirty years is a long time."

Behind us the line was starting to grow anxious. Several people shouted at the guard to speed it up.

The young man glanced around us and returned the shouts with a rude gesture. "Sorry about that. Well you folks enjoy your visit. And stay out of trouble, all right?" He handed Hazel her papers and stepped aside, letting us through.

I watched him for a moment as we passed, but I was pretty quickly distracted as the city came into view.

I'd seen bigger buildings in my life, but for some reason I was still impressed. As far as I could see was brick and stone. The same wall that enclosed the courtyard spread out in either direction and I guessed that it probably wrapped around the entire city. Just like the last town we'd visited.

Every building along the street was stone and stood several stories high. Signs displaying colorful mascots and letters I didn't recognize hung over doors. In alleyways there were booths and tents with merchants shouting and waving wares.

Even the street was enough to impress me. The cobbles seemed as smooth as a freshly paved street from back home.

The people reminded me a lot of those we'd seen back in Amethyst Lake, but there were so many more of them! And for every ten people dressed in plain clothes there was one in chain or plate mail. Occasionally I even saw someone dressed all in silk, chin lifted as they ignored the masses around them.

Hazel followed Arthur down the street until he found a mostly empty alley and stepped out of the flow of traffic.

"You okay?" he asked Hazel.

She nodded, though even I noticed how nervous the crowd had made her.

"Do you have any idea where you plan on staying?"

Her eyes widened in sudden panic and she shook her head.

"Okay. I think I know a good place. If it's still open, that is. Follow me."

He led us back out into the street.

The streets of Glanzend felt more organized than the ones in Amethyst Lake. They ran straight instead of winding around haphazardly.

Arthur led us down those roads, turning occasionally, until he stopped in front of a stone building, slightly larger than its neighbors.

A wooden sign swung over the door, the face of a dog grinning down at us.

"The Robber's Dog?" Hazel asked.

"It's—well, used to be—one of the most discrete inns in the city. If nothing else, they have beds. And that has to be better than a cart bench." He went inside and Hazel followed.

Once over the threshold Hazel put me down. I felt a little guilty as I watched her rub her shoulder before holding out a hand for me.

The two of us waited as Arthur spoke with the man behind the front desk. The man nodded when Arthur pointed at us. Arthur passed a handful of coins over in exchange for a key.

Arthur came back to us and handed Hazel the key. "Room five, second floor."

"So, now what?" Hazel asked.

"Now, you two make yourselves comfortable. I'm going home."

For a second I thought I heard his voice break, but I knew that couldn't be true.

———

There is indeed a statue of him outside the temple. Twenty years younger—thirty by the reasoning of anyone in this world—and with a chin more square than any man could actually have, but it is of him. The plaque on the base says so.

"Arthur Shield. First Knight. Hero. Fallen Brother."

He feels ill as he stares at it. This slab of granite is meant to honor his life. A life he is no longer sure has any honor left.

He glances around at the busy square, suddenly self-conscious. No one takes notice of him.

Arthur remembers when this area had just been an empty lot. Cobbled gray stone had filled the area, its sole purpose as a parade ground for any time the knights of Saban had felt the need to give a demonstration of their power.

Now it's a park. He almost can't believe it. Green grass and trees fill the area, and in one corner, the farthest from the street in front of the temple, is a small wooden castle.

He watches for a short time, the children that climb it

and claim their lordship over the park. High, loud voices laugh and scream in a way he has never been used to.

He pushes the children from his mind. There is only one child he needs to worry about right now. And his only concern is to get her out of his life.

Just across the street rises the wall. Taller even than the city's walls, with a massive iron gate. Flags flutter on top of the wall, blue and gray, and armored men and woman patrol, spear tips catching the autumn sunlight.

The temple's compound is on the western edge of Glanzend. Its walls practically touching the city's. Inside it is another city. There are barracks and homes for members of the order, craftsman and artisans to see to whatever the knights might need. Training grounds and amphitheater.

Arthur wonders, idly, how the amphitheater is used now. It had once been where Saban would speak to his knights. Would instruct and teach. Where new knights would gain their armor and where Saban would grant them their power.

Arthur flexes a rough hand. He misses that power. Not as much as he misses Saban, but he misses the power. The blue flames that turned the guilty to ash, the mystical armor, the strength.

That all died with his god.

"Can gods die?" he asks himself again.

He almost turns away from the gate, but he is driven forward. He has to know. Has to see how they have fared. He has only lived with the knowledge of his god's death for months, his fellows have lived with it for ten years. How would that change them?

Compared to the rest of the city, the street before the temple is practically empty. Even with the park so close, the citizens of the city avoid the compound. They always have. Arthur has always assumed it was from a fear of justice.

"Justice is dead," he says to himself as he crosses the street.

He stops in front of the small door next to the portcullis. He steels himself and knocks on the door.

A small window, at eye level, slides open and a pair of impatient eyes stare out. "What's your business here, sir?" Despite the honorific, there is no respect in the voice.

He is at a loss for words. He has practiced this moment in his head for nearly twenty years, but he now has no words to say.

"Sir?"

"I'm...my name is Arthur Shield. I once served Saban." These were not the words he wanted to say, and not spoken so clumsily, but he has said it. He waits for the response.

It seems to take longer in coming than he would have expected. "Sir, I have to say, that I don't appreciate your joke."

"No joke. I am Arthur Shield. I'm here to see...shit, I don't even know who resides in the temple anymore. I need to speak to someone in charge?"

"Do you have an appointment?"

"No, I—"

"Then I recommend you contact someone in your local guard station and ask them to make an appointment for you."

Arthur flips his cloak back to reveal the sword at his side. He gestures, almost frantically, to the symbol on the pommel. "Please, look, I need to get inside."

The eyes lock on the sword. "Where did you get that?" Hostile, angry.

"It's mine. It was gifted to me by Saban himself. Please,

I just need to speak to someone in charge." He is surprised at the pleading in his own voice.

The window closes. Through the portcullis he sees the man rushing off, and almost immediately returning, followed by a large group of other men. All are dressed in armor and carry weapons.

He takes a step back away from the wall and waits. The gate is opened with impressive speed and the group of armed men surround him.

He feels a small bit of pride to find that the order is still efficient.

"What is your name?" A man, possibly in his thirties, demands.

"As I told your brother, my name is Arthur Shield." Arthur stands straighter, hoping to give a good first impression to his younger brothers.

"Show me the sword," the man orders.

"Are you a commander?" Arthur asks as he draws his weapon and holds it hilt first toward the man.

There is an audible gasp from the men at the sight of the broken sword as it clears its scabbard.

The man wrenches the weapon away from Arthur. The tip catches the old man's hand, but he refrains from crying out as blood wells up in his palm. "I am Commander Roderick Clay. I command the forces of this temple. You will come with us. Whoever you are."

"I told you. I am Arthur Shield."

Clay's face twists in disgust. "How dare you?" He stares down at the sword with almost reverence before shouting to his men. "Bind him. He will tell us who he is."

Arthur does not fight as his feet are swept from under him and his arms twisted behind his back. "There must be someone who can vouch for me?" he asks, but none respond.

Before he can ask again, a sword hilt is smashed into his head and he loses consciousness.

———

"I'm bored," I announced to the room. Hazel was the only other occupant, but it was really her decision if she chose to listen to me or not.

She had been lost in her own world for most of the morning. She sat cross-legged on her bed with a small, leather-bound book open in her lap and the small, bone-white twig resting in front of her.

While ignoring me, she was mumbling to herself. "I could use that spell. Should be strong enough to stop almost anything. But a hag? How do I even know we'll see her again? Oh, who am I kidding? She'll be back." She flipped several pages in her book and stopped. "Oh, that one's good. Hm, but the range. That could be a problem. Have to be right in front of them for it to work. Still, probably worth it. Can probably only fit one charge of it, though."

In the few days we'd been holed up in the room I'd gotten used to Hazel talking to herself. I suspected that she didn't always realize she was doing it. Usually, I enjoyed listening because she usually talked about her magic. I didn't fully understand it, but I'd been able to determine that her magic worked by her casting spells and storing them in her little wand. I wanted to ask her about it but I was also scared to. I'd seen what her magic could do and really didn't want to remember that morning on the cart.

I spoke up again, louder this time. "I'm bored."

She looked up from her book. "I'm sorry, sweetie. What would you like to do?"

I'd almost expected her to continue ignoring me. I slid off my bed and bounced over to hers. Climbing up next to her, I shrugged. "I don't know. What's there to do here?"

I asked this question every time she asked me what I wanted to do. Usually all she managed to come up with was a walk out in the city, which I usually jumped at. In the days we'd been waiting for Arthur to return I'd not grown tired of the stone city outside our room. All the different people, the gnomes, dwarves, even the rare elf.

Hazel insisted that Glanzend was one of the most xenophobic—I'd needed her to explain that word for me— cities in the country. "Any other city and you see so many other different people, Miki."

"Other orcs?" I'd asked.

She'd just smiled and nodded.

I really wanted to get back out and do some more people watching. The last time we'd gone outside I'd noticed that Hazel seemed very nervous. When I'd asked what was wrong she'd just shaken her head and turned us back around toward the inn. Because of that I didn't want to be the one to suggest we go outside again. I had thought that maybe she was still having trouble with the crowds, but I was starting to suspect that she might be worried about Arthur.

"Well," she looked from me to the closed window above her bed. The shutters allowed only a fraction of the city's noise to filter through.

"We don't have to go outside if you don't want to, Hazel," I said, feeling very generous in giving her this out.

"Oh, really?" She grinned down at me.

I nodded. "It's okay if you don't like big crowds. I have cousins that don't like going out in big groups either."

"Tell me about your cousins." She closed her book and rested on an elbow, waiting for me to talk.

"Well, they're not really cousins, but dad always says that they're basically family, so I should treat them like it. Even if they're just goblins."

"Goblins?" Hazel's eyebrows went up in surprise.

I nodded. "Yeah. Uncle Jack's mom's a goblin. She's kinda the leader of all the goblins in town. They don't like going outside too much, because most people stare at them. They make good food though."

"Do they cook for you a lot?"

I nodded. "Dad likes to take me to Jack's Place. It's a diner in town. Everybody loves it."

"Does your Uncle Jack run it?" she asked.

I gave her an incredulous look. "No. His grandpa does. It's not named after him, though. A lot of my uncles are named Jack, actually. They're all named after the wizard that saved them."

"A wizard named Jack? That's a funny name for a wizard."

"Is it?"

"It's just a funny name. And you say a lot of your uncles are named that?"

"Yeah. But Uncle Jack is the best one. He's always nice to me." I fell quiet, suddenly missing my family again.

Hazel patted my arm gently. "What did you say your mother's name was, Miki?"

"Lise," I answered.

"Not a very orcish name. Though I guess neither is Jack."

"Oh, mom's human. Daddy's a orc."

"You said your name was Goretusk, though?"

I nodded.

"You didn't take your mother's name? Isn't that how it works with orcs?"

I shrugged. "My mom argued with gramma about that once. Said, *well in this country a child takes their father's name.*" I did my best to imitate my mother's voice. "Gramma was upset about that, but I think she was also a little happy that I had the same name as her."

"Her name was Mikaia, too?"

I shook my head. "No. Her name was Karen. Well, her real name was Shakill."

Hazel sat up straight. "Hang on. Your grandmother was named Shakill Goretusk?"

I nodded, the more I talked about my family the happier I was growing.

"And your Uncle, is he a Goretusk, too? No, you said his mother was a goblin..." she trailed off, lost in thought.

"Uncle Jack's mom doesn't have a last name, so he got his dad's. Bloodfist."

Hazel spun on me. "Is his father's name Garack Bloodfist?"

"I think? Everyone called him Gary, but I never knew him. I was only a baby when he died."

She sank back down into her bed. "He's dead?"

"Did you know him?" I asked, oblivious to the fact that it would be impossible for Hazel to know Jack's father.

She shook her head. "No. But I've heard stories about him. I have a friend who always wanted to meet him." She suddenly seemed very sad.

"I'm sorry, Hazel." I scooted closer and hugged her arm. "I didn't mean to make you sad."

"Oh, sweetie, you didn't make me sad." She wrapped her free arm around me.

"Ok." I didn't say anything else, just sat in the hug.

"What do you say we go for another walk?"

"Really?" I looked up, excited.

Hazel nodded and put her book down, picking up another. She'd bought the second book from a store on our first expedition into the city. "Yup, I've been reading up on the city and I think I can get us around more easily."

"Where are we gonna go?" I asked, bouncing up and down, still holding her arm in a death-grip.

"Hey, hey, let go." She laughed as she shook me off her arm.

I bounced up and caught it again, laughing with her. "Where we going? Where we going?"

"How would you like to see where Arthur went?" she asked.

"Really?"

"Sure. What's the worst that can happen?"

I didn't quite understand what she meant but answered anyway. "Nothing."

"Exactly!"

She jumped off the bed and gathered up our coats.

CHAINS

THREE YEARS Ago
   Upstate New York

"Still with us, Arty?" The man asks.

Arthur Shield stirs from his revery and looks across at the short man. Bert is his name. Arthur doesn't like him. He's far too familiar with everybody. Arthur knows his type. A killer.

Arthur is a killer, too, but not the same kind. He has only ever killed on behalf of Justice. Bert has killed simply because he's good at it. It's that talent for killing that earned Bert a seat across from Shield in this truck.

He and the other man sitting next to Arthur. Arthur likes that one more. He doesn't talk as much. Vladik. The man is almost as large as an orc, and Arthur knows firsthand that the man can use that size well.

"Not gonna answer me?" Bert asks.

Arthur looks away, wishing for a window in the back of the truck. Since there isn't one he just stares at the small square of mesh in the wall that divides the three of them from the driver and their team's leader.

"Fine. Get back to your prayin' then, old man."

Arthur does just that. It is all he ever does. For seventeen years, it is all he's done. He has never received an answer, but he knows his god, Saban, is searching for him too. He has to be.

"We're here," Leanora shouts through the screen at the three men in the back. "Get ready."

They comply. Strapped-on vests are tightened, magazines double checked, gun stocks adjusted. Arthur feels a pang of regret that he has grown accustomed to the gear he now uses. He misses his plate armor, his sword, his magic.

It wasn't really his magic. It was Saban's. But the god shares his power with his knights. Arthur knows that if Saban would find him, once again share his strength, he would be able to complete the mission he'd been given. He would be able to break the spell that binds him to Leanora, that forces him to obey her orders. He would be able to escape his concrete prison and hunt down Bloodfist and the rest of the orcs that had defiled his home.

The truck stops. The front doors open and the three men in the back rise to their feet in preparation for the back doors to open.

Umanand opens the back door with one hand. The other has a rifle trained at a house situated in the middle of an empty field.

Vladik exits the truck first, gun up and sweeping the area as he drops to the ground. Burt goes next, doing the same. Arthur steps out of the truck, gun hanging casually at his side. He scans the area with a bored expression. He hears no violence.

"Can you take this seriously for once, Arthur?" Leanora demands of him. She carries no weapons. She doesn't need any. Arthur has seen what her magic can do. He thinks that she might even be a challenge for him if he had his powers back.

"I thought you said we were marching into a war zone, boss." Burt says.

"Looks like we missed the war. I'm sensing some residual energy, though. Be on alert. If you find any survivors, do your best to keep them as survivors. We need to know what happened."

Vladik sniffs the air. "Witches."

Arthur is surprised by the declaration and stops his bored study of the farmland to consider the tall blond man. "Why do you say that?"

"I can smell their magic. Dirty. Like," he waves a hand desperately, as he tries to make the comparison, "Like turned potato."

Burt takes a deep breath through his nose before giving Vladik a concerned look. "All I smell is cow shit, man."

"That too," Vladik agrees.

Leanora nods. "Vlad's right. It has to be witches. Whatever spell that was cast here must have taken months of preparation. Be careful. We still have no idea what was going on, and whatever that spell was meant to do has already been done."

"I thought the company was supposed to be able to preemptively stop this sort of thing?" Burt says as he falls in line behind Umanand.

"Shut up." Leanora's voice carries a wave of power with it.

Arthur can feel the small amulet around his neck as it burns the order into him. The mission has officially started.

The wizard has used her power and now her squad must obey her orders or her magic will tear them apart from the inside.

The five of them pass through a short, whitewashed gate that is swinging in the wind. As they cross the line, Arthur can feel the ward. Even without his power he can recognize the magic. The protective circle has already been broken, he can tell that much, but it must have been a powerful ward to linger at all, let alone with that much power.

Leanora uses hand signals, silently ordering her team to spread out. The farm isn't very large. Not compared to some Arthur has seen, but he can tell that it had housed many people at one time. It has the sense of a well lived in space.

There are two barns, a large greenhouse, several pens with coops or stables, and a spread-out three-story farmhouse.

Leanora sends Arthur toward the farmhouse.

He spots the first body the instant he turns toward the building. The woman is splayed out on the front porch. At the sight of her blood he finally shoulders his rifle and falls into a shooting stance. He stalks, body low and gun ready, toward the house.

When he arrives he inspects the body after flipping her over onto her back with a boot. The woman had been old. He would guess in her seventies, possibly older. Her stomach has been torn open. He knows this to be true even though her green polka-dotted dress has not been damaged, only drenched through from the contents of the woman's stomach. He knows the smell of a disemboweling. Her bloated face is stuck in a twisted mask of pain.

He finds the next body on the other side of the open door. He can see the wound on this one. Blood has pooled around her from an opening in her neck. A cursory glance tells Arthur that the weapon went completely through the neck. It wasn't a traditional blade. The wound is round, not a long gash.

His stomach clenches. Not from the gore, he's too used to this. It's an unexpected fear growing inside him. These kills were done with magic. In the years he's been forced to serve his current taskmasters he's fought several magic users, but it's usually more mundane enemies. No one has believed him the few times he's mentioned his former power, so he is usually only sent against "norms," as they like to call them. Now he feels a slightly unpleasant thrill at the prospect of another sort of fight.

A sound from above causes him to turn from the body. He keeps himself composed. He's been through worse, he's sure of it.

He leaves the dead woman and heads toward the stairs. The farmhouse is a disaster. Shattered glass and overturned furniture litter the living room. Another body lies at the top of the first flight of stairs. Arthur takes his time to avoid stepping in the river of coagulated blood that runs down to the ground floor.

He stops at the top of the stairs and pauses at the first corner in a hallway. Glancing around, he sees two more dead women, one at each end of the passageway. All the doors in the hall are wide open, save one. Arthur is confident that is where the sound came from.

Despite his size and age Arthur is silent as he covers the distance. He goes slowly, successfully avoiding creaking floorboards and the blood and limbs of the dead.

He avoids standing in front of the closed door to ensure his shadow doesn't fall over the crack at the bottom.

He closes his eyes and listens. He doesn't have to strain his ears. He could hear the crying before he even reached the door. He guesses it's a survivor of the massacre.

If Vladik is correct about this being the work of witches, it was likely some powerful witch-hunters had torn through the farm, had broken the witches ward, and gone to work.

The sobs on the other side of the door are pained. Arthur suspects they hadn't escaped without any injuries. Hopefully that means he can capture them without too much effort.

He reaches out with one hand and turns the knob. The door is unlocked.

The crying stops and Arthur moves. He throws the door open and turns into the room, gun sweeping left to right and back again.

A girl sits on the floor next to a simple bed. Her face is speckled with blood, cleaned by tears that still pour from her eyes.

The crying eyes open wide with fear at the sight of Arthur. The girl scrambles onto the bed and begins to crawl toward the window over the headrest.

"Stop." Arthur's voice is calm but forceful.

The girl stops and glances over at him. "Please don't hurt me," she begs.

She is young, maybe thirteen, though Arthur has never been good at guessing the age of children. "I won't if you don't give me a reason to. Now sit back down."

The girl complies, sitting on the bed. She wipes a stained sleeve over her face, smearing the blood and tears further.

"What happened here?" Arthur asks. He really shouldn't be the one asking the questions, but he's curious. The killing was done by a professional. He's sure of that. He wants to know how this girl escaped. He can see no wounds on her. The blood that covers her seems to have come from someone else, meaning she was present when the killing started, but had somehow escaped.

"They're all dead," she says.

"I can see that. How did you escape?"

The girl looks up in surprise. "You're not here to arrest me?"

"Arrest..." Arthur suddenly realizes why she is unhurt. "You did all that?" He points out the door, the foot of a dead woman is visible.

The girl looks back down, seemingly ashamed. "I had to."

Arthur scowls. "Why?"

"They were going to kill everyone." She looks up, meeting his gaze. Her eyes hold a strength that surprises him, though seeing what she has done, it probably shouldn't. "The town. They were going to sacrifice the whole town. When I found out, I... I knew I had to do something."

"How did you—"

Before he can finish his question the radio strapped to his shoulder crackles, "Arthur, we've found nothing but dead old women. You find anything interesting on your end?" Leonora's voice asks.

Arthur raises a finger at the girl, telling her to wait, and responds. "Found a survivor. Second story of the house."

"Roger. On our way."

He turns his attention back to the girl. "How did you do all this?" It is only curiosity. Seventeen years ago he might have been concerned by the dead. Or he might have praised the girl for her work in saving lives by killing witches. He would have requested to oversee the trial, at least. But now he is merely curious.

She looks away, shyly. "What's going to happen to me?"

He shakes his head. "Not my decision. Answer my question, girl."

"Magic," she mumbles her response.

"Magic?" he asks.

"You don't have to believe me, okay? But they were witches. I'm a witch. But... I don't... I don't want to be like them."

"I believe you." The tight ball of fear in his gut has vanished and he lowers his gun, letting it hang at his side. "Mind if I sit?" He indicates a small chair in front of a small desk.

She opens her mouth to speak, but just nods instead.

"Thank you." He sighs as he sits down. "I have to tell you, I was sure that all this was the work of a professional."

"Professional?" she asks.

He nods. "I'm Arthur."

"I'm Melody."

"Nice to meet you Melody. My teammates will be here soon. You're going to be in trouble for what happened here, you know that, right?"

"But I saved everyone."

Arthur shrugs. "I believe you, but you're apparently an incredibly powerful magic user. That's something my... employers? Yeah, employers. It's something they value very highly."

"What do you mean?"

"I suspect we'll be working together in the future."

She studies him, eyes narrowing in suspicion. "I'm just a kid."

"Don't worry. I'm just an old man. Things like that don't stop them."

"How's that fair?" she asks.

"It's not. But in my time here I've come to find that

there is very little justice in this world. Maybe one day that will change." He rises from his seat in time to greet Leanora.

The wizard questions the girl and they leave the farm.

There is no window in the back of the truck, so none of them can see the fire. Melody can. She sits in the front with Leanora, a small bag in her lap.

She accepted Leanora's offer for a job. Arthur has never known anyone to refuse.

———

I was too excited at the sight of the park to be angry with Hazel. I felt like I should be angry that we hadn't come here every day while we waited to hear from Arthur, but the sight of the wooden castle drove all those thoughts out of my head.

I let out a squealing roar of excitement and charged across the yellowing grass to join the horde of other children already scaling the walls of the tiny fortress.

"Be careful!" Hazel shouted after I tore myself free of her grip.

I glanced over my shoulder long enough to grin widely at her. I caught her expression and closed my mouth, suddenly self-conscious of my small tusks.

I forgot that concern almost as quickly as it had entered my mind once I reached the playground.

The slatted wood of the play-castle was covered in handholds allowing me to climb to the top without much issue.

Once I reached the top I was greeted by a defending force of comically serious boys.

One of them held up his hand and stared at me from

behind a curtain of curly blond hair. "Which army are you with?" he demanded.

I considered his question very seriously for a moment. "Which army are *you* with?" I answered.

The group glanced at each other, surprised by the sudden shift in power. "We're the Knights of Saban." The blond boy puffed his chest out and pointed behind himself.

I followed his finger to the massive gray walls across the street from the park. Blue banners fluttered in a cold wind. Hazel had told me that was where Arthur was. Arthur was a Knight of Saban, I was pretty sure of that. I liked Arthur, even if he wasn't the friendliest person I'd ever met. Maybe I could be a Knight of Saban, too?

"Me too," I answered.

They seemed taken aback by my declaration and consulted with each other briefly. As they did so, countless other children swarmed around me and into the castle.

I sat down on the battlement while I waited for them to reach a decision. I glanced around at the park. From the impressive six feet up I felt I could see everything.

I spotted Hazel, sitting on a bench and talking to another woman. The other woman seemed tired and carried a baby in her arms. I waved at Hazel, who glanced up long enough to wave back before returning to her conversation.

"Okay. We decided that you can be a Knight of Saban."

"Really?" I asked, excited.

"Yeah. But only if you defend the wall while we go on the slide."

"Okay." I was too excited to argue.

The boys all grinned and rushed off across a small rope bridge that led to a metal slide.

I abandoned my post almost immediately. I spotted

swings off in the distance. I went down the slide and hit the ground running.

I was still slowly coming to terms with the fact that I wasn't on Earth anymore, but that didn't matter to me at that moment, because apparently every world had the same sort of playground equipment.

I had just got the swing to the perfect arc to launch myself into the air when somebody grabbed the chain and stopped me.

I glanced up, irritated, to find Hazel.

"We have to go." She held out her hand for me and I accepted it.

"Why?" I asked.

"Just come on." She began to walk across the grass, dragging me behind her. She kept glancing over her shoulder and I mimicked her action.

It took me a while to see what she was looking for, but the street in front of the temple of Saban was almost completely empty, so it only took a little while for me to see the familiar face right before it turned to face the door.

The elf, Lara, raised a fist and pounded on the door.

————

The manacles bite into Arthur's skin as he is once again led from his cell into one of the temple's many judgement halls.

A paladin in full battle dress rises and steps up to the podium at the head of the long room. "Ready to tell us your real name, imposter?"

There is a chorus of angry murmurs from the rest of the gathered knights.

"I have told you my name, Paladin Clay," Arthur answers.

JAMES JAKINS

"You continue to insist that you are Arthur Shield?" Roderick Clay asks.

The man is young. Very young to be an arbiter. Possibly even younger than Arthur himself was when he first obtained the rank.

Arthur learned after years in the position, that young men were not always the best choice for such authority. He, at least, had been lucky enough to have Saban himself teach him how to judge justly. He supposed that Roderick Clay might have been a capable paladin—he must be to have moved up the ranks so fast—but Arthur can't help but feel a severe dislike for the man. Being chained and questioned every day for a week has that effect on a man.

Arthur doesn't even try to stifle the exasperated sigh. "I *am* Arthur Shield. Surely someone must still live who knew me."

Clay studies Arthur. As he does he taps his fingers restlessly on the podium. The sound of his steel-gloved fingers can be heard even over the angry conversations of the audience.

A man claiming to be Arthur Shield was big news in the temple, and every day when he was brought before Clay to be questioned a crowd gathered. Most were respectful and said nothing as Clay asked his pointless questions. Sometimes, though, a man would lose his patience and shout an obscenity at Arthur. He would then be escorted out of the room by his fellows.

Arthur almost feels proud of this. His name must truly be loved here for them to react in this way. Or, perhaps, it is because they all secretly know that Arthur Shield is the one responsible for Saban's death and they want to make sure it is really him before they execute him.

He is only surprised that the order's so-called prophet

94

has never made an appearance. When he has asked after the man, none of the knights would answer. Apparently, the man who now speaks for Saban doesn't even live in the temple.

So, it is Roderick Clay that Arthur has to convince.

"Arthur Shield would not speak the blasphemies you have spoken, sir." Clay steps around the podium and approaches the center of the room, where Arthur is chained to the floor.

His nose twists in distaste as he gets closer. Arthur has not been allowed a washbasin his entire time being imprisoned.

"Saban taught me that the truth is never blasphemy," Arthur answers.

"Oh, is this the same Saban you claim is dead?" Clay pushes past his obvious discomfort at Arthur's scent and sticks his face right up to Arthur's, no longer hiding any of his anger.

"The same."

The room erupts in a cacophony of anger.

Clay raises a hand and the shouting dies down. "What evidence do you have of this death?"

Arthur raises his eyes for the first time, he hopes his expression is calm, understanding. He does not want to hurt these men. They would be his brothers, if only he still considered himself worthy of the title. "Tell me, Paladin Clay, can you summon the power of Saban?"

Some of the men in the crowd shout again, but from the corner of his eye Arthur notices several of the older knights exchanging glances.

"No." The admission from Clay surprises Arthur. The young man has been so adamant in his convictions this past week that Arthur almost expected denial. "But that is only because he does not feel it necessary for one of my calling."

"You know that's not true," Arthur tries to step forward but his chains stop him. "Any found worthy to wield a sword in his name is granted that power." He glances around, hoping to see acknowledgement in the eyes of the others, but he finds only anger.

Clay coughs an angry laugh and returns to the podium. "It doesn't matter. We're not on trial. You are. For stealing the identity of one of our order's noblest."

Arthur drops his head again. Noble? If only these men knew what he really was. Maybe he had been noble once, but that man was dead. Now he is just a killer. A dog to be pointed and unleashed.

A thought crosses his mind and he physically cringes as it passes. *You've always been nothing more than a dog. Only your master changed.*

"But," Clay continues, "You should be happy."

Arthur looks up at that strange statement to find a cruel smile breaking Clay's square face. "We found one of your old, uh, *friends*. You will of course remember Paladin Victor Kraken."

Arthur's face lights up at the name. The gathered crowd's murmuring changes tone at this.

"Victor? He's still alive? But he must be," he pauses to do the math in his head, "What? Ninety, now?"

Clay's brows furrow. "Yes, he is in his ninety-fifth year. You've done your homework, haven't you, imposter?"

Arthur swallows the angry retort that rises. "Victor is one of my oldest friends. I served as his squire for a time."

"He did tell us that Arthur Shield had been his squire, this is true."

"Where is he?" Arthur asks.

"He will be here the day after tomorrow. He has retired outside of Glanzend. But he has agreed to testify, for or against you. His testimony will determine your fate."

Arthur's shoulders slump in relief. "Thank you."

Clay barks another laugh. "We don't do this for you. We must prove without a doubt your guilt before we sentence you."

Arthur nods and his chains rattle. "Of course."

"But even if you are Shield," Clay's eyes bore through Arthur, "you have spoken blasphemy against your own god. Do you think that can be forgiven?"

Arthur shakes his head. "I only speak truth, but I do expect punishment for my part in his death."

The gathered whisper again but he and Clay ignore them.

A young squire rushes into the room and up to the podium. Roderick bends to hear the urgently whispered message. He rises and smiles at Arthur as he answers the boy. "Thank you. Send her in."

Arthur feels a familiar fear grip his gut. Have they found them? He hasn't mentioned the girls, but witnesses would have seen him traveling with them. Despite himself he has come to care about them both, both the orc and the witch. He knows it would be easier if they were gone, if he just turned them over for judgement, but he can't.

Hazel reminds him of Melody, even if only because of her witchcraft. And Mikaia... the child of a sworn enemy. A tiny monster that his god had demanded he kill.

No. She is just a child. A child that trusts him. A child he has made a promise to protect. Yes, given the chance, he would kill the man that promise was made to. That doesn't change that he gave his word. It is all he has. Isn't it?

He turns his head—the only part of his body not

chained in place—to find another familiar face being led inside the long chamber.

Her name is Lara. He remembers that much. The elf gives him a satisfied smirk as she passes him.

"Madam Elf." Roderick steps from behind the podium and offers a shallow bow. "I believe you have come to testify against our prisoner."

"I have." She doesn't look at Clay, but instead glares at Arthur with more murderous intent than he has felt in a long time.

"Please, tell us of his crimes."

She obliges. She tells them everything. From finding Arthur and Miki on the side of the road to his defeating her and her rabble in the inn. Arthur does not look away. Even when she names Mikaia as orc.

"Goretusk? You're sure?" Clay asks, once the story is told.

"That is the name she herself told me." Lara's grin is victorious.

Clay turns to Arthur. "What do you have to say for yourself? If nothing else, this proves you are not who you claim to be."

"I promised to protect her." The argument sounds weak to his ears, but it is his reason.

"Promised who?"

"She's only a child," Arthur continues, ignoring the question.

"The child of a heretic. A monster. Now answer my question. Who did you promise? What enemy of this temple are you working for?"

Arthur shakes his head and sighs again. No point in lying about it. "His name is Garack Bloodfist. The second of his name. The man who murdered Saban."

And he'd thought the cursing had been bad before.

———

Three Years Ago
Brown Roost, Western Aanfang

"There is no shame in this, girl." The old woman's voice is gentle, soothing, but the edges of her words are sharpened with urgency.

Hazel Midd shakes her head. "I know, but..."

"You wish to keep the child?" The hand working the pestle stops, herbs left half-crushed.

"I... I don't know."

"Then why come to me?" There is no reproach in the question. This old woman, known only as Yilda, has lived outside the village of Brown Roost for longer than anyone can remember. This service is one she has provided for many.

"I wish to keep the child. It's a girl," Hazel admits to herself and the woman.

Yilda narrows her eyes at this declaration. "How would you know, girl?"

"I... I just do."

Yilda shrugs. "So be it, but why come to me?"

Hazel forces her fear down and answers. "There are rumors, in town, that you are not just a medicine woman."

Yilda raises her gray brows at this. "Oh?"

"I want to make him pay. For what he took from me. For what he's done to all the other women."

Yilda shakes her head mournfully. "He is the lord of this

village. The Empress herself has granted his family dominion over this land."

"How does that make this okay?" Hazel slams her hands on the table and rises to her feet. "How can that possibly excuse what he did? What he does?" Her voice quavers, but less of that is anger than she likes.

"What would you do, girl? How would you make him pay?" Yilda studies the young woman, eyes peering beyond the bloodless, shaking hands, through the eyes lit with anger and fear.

"Magic. You're a witch, I know you are."

"Says who?"

"Everyone. Everyone knows it."

"Witchcraft is illegal within the empire, Miss Midd. You know that."

"Hasn't stopped you."

"What I do is not witchcraft. It is alchemy," she waves at the mortar and pestle and the half-formed paste, "nothing more."

"He has to be stopped. Please?" Hazel falls back to her seat and clasps her still-shaking hands together. "I beg you. You must be able to show me something."

"No, child. This road is not one you should walk. If you do not want my medicine, you should leave." Yilda turns from Hazel, rising from her own seat and shambling away. "I will be in my garden, should you change your mind." She glances at Hazel and then looks to a bookcase on the far wall. When she glances back to the girl she nods.

The medicine woman's back door opens and closes, leaving Hazel alone.

She rises and approaches the bookshelf. At first she is not sure what she is supposed to find, but she recognizes it instinctually. A small book bound in a pale leather. There is no title on the cover and when she opens it she discovers that its contents are written by hand. The early pages in a blocky, utilitarian text. As it progresses the letters evolve into a flowing, practiced hand. The final passages, before the pages are revealed to be blank, are shaky and difficult to interpret.

She takes the book and leaves the witch's hut.

It takes her months to learn what she needs to. Her body is betraying the secret she has tried to keep by the time she is ready.

She sends a messenger and arranges a meeting at the local tavern. He is waiting for her when she arrives.

He sneers up at her as she approaches the table and sits down.

She hangs her head low, the shame he has put her through burning her face and twisting her insides. The unborn child a reminder of his violation. But he is a lord. It was his right. Her own brother has made that declaration.

"Come to ask for help?" The man asks. "Do you wish to legitimize my little bastard before it's even born?" His tone makes it plain that he would never do that. This monster has more children in the village than any would acknowledge.

Hazel hates him. All the women fear him. And the men pretend that no wrong has been committed.

Hazel pulls the wand from her robe, hidden by the table top, and aims it at the man. She has crafted the bone white length of wood for this sole purpose. Has charged it with months' worth of labor.

"No," she answers finally, forcing as much steel into her voice as she can.

"Then what? Want another go? Back in the field maybe?" His sneer grows. "Maybe one of my boys can have a turn this time?" He waves magnanimously at the table behind him, filled with men in boiled leather carrying chipped swords.

She says the word. The silent command of her spell. Its range is barely the length of the table, but it does what she has hoped it would.

One instant the man is there, sneering at her and laughing with the thugs that pretend to be knights, and then there is a red mist and the sound of wet chunks of meat raining around them.

The men curse and rise, some thinking to draw swords, others tripping over themselves to rush away.

Hazel has already stood and taken the few steps necessary. She says the word again, silent and painful, and the lord's entourage is no more.

She burns the tavern down before she leaves.

Outside, lit by the growing fire, she retrieves the bag she had left on the side of the muddy street. It is everything she has left in the world.

She does not return home. She never will. She will never regret her decision.

PLANS

I was nervous. I had no idea why, other than the fact that Hazel hadn't stopped pacing for what had felt like days. It had really only been a few hours, but the way she was chewing on her thumbnail and muttering to herself made it seem really bad.

Not for the first time, I asked the question, "What's wrong, Hazel?"

"Nothing, sweetie," she lied, again.

"Are you worried that the elf lady is going to try to hurt Arthur again?"

She stopped and considered me, what was left of her left thumb's nail slowly shrinking between her teeth. "You're pretty smart for a kid."

"Thanks."

She smiled at me before returning to her pacing. "What do I do?" she asked the room.

Since there was no one else there, I answered. "Should we go get him back?"

She shook her head. "How could we do that?"

I shrugged. "I dunno. Climb the walls?"

Hazel laughed at that. "Right. I'm sure that would work. Besides, we don't even know if he's alive. Oh, who am I kidding? Of course he is. But can I still trust him? Maybe? I mean... he would have turned us in already, right? Why hasn't he come back? Or turned us in? What is going on?" She was talking really fast, her free hand waving in front of her, as though she were conducting some unseen music. She stopped and flopped down onto the bed. "Ah! We have to get in there. Well," she sat up and looked at me. "I have to get in there. We need to find somewhere safe for you."

"I want to come. I want to see the place Arthur grew up."

"Who told you he grew up there?" she asked.

I shrugged again. "He seemed really excited to go back. And I heard some of the kids at the park talking about how knights grow up in the temple. One kid said his mom is a washer in there and that she was going to get him a job as a square or something."

"Squire," she corrected. Then she sat bolt upright. "His mother's a washer?"

"That's what he said."

She rose again and began pacing anew. This time both hands waved excitedly as she talked with herself. "Of course they'd have washers. It's practically a whole gods-damned city in there. They probably constantly need people. I bet they're always looking for women to do laundry or mop the floors. Maybe I could get a job? Yeah. I'm sure I could. Ryta always tells me I look like a maid. Then, I can get in, look around without anyone getting suspicious. Maybe I could find her? See what happened to the old man. But what do I do about Miki? I can't leave her alone. But can I take her in with me?"

"I wanna go," I said over her.

She ignored me and continued her one-sided conversation. "I'll have to ask around. Maybe they have somewhere for children. But will she be safe?" She stopped and looked at me again.

I nodded, answering her question for her.

"Think you can be a good girl for me for a little while? I need to run out for a bit."

I pouted but nodded in agreement.

"Great. Lock the door behind me and don't open it for anybody. Okay?"

Again, I nodded, trying my best to convey my disappointment in being forced to stay behind.

"Thank you. I'll bring you back something nice. How does a cake sound?"

"A whole cake?" I sat up, excited at this prospect.

"Well, it'll be small, but you can have all of it."

I considered. A small cake was better than no cake. "Okay."

"Perfect. I'll be back soon." She grabbed her cloak and bag and rushed out the door.

I did as she bid and locked it behind her. I have no idea how I managed to keep myself entertained in that empty room while I waited for her to return.

When she finally did get back I almost didn't hear her knocking and calling for me. I crawled out from under the fort I'd made of the room's two scratchy mattresses and slid the bolt open.

She pushed in. "Did you fall asleep? What took you so long..." she trailed off as she stared at my handiwork. "How did you get the bedside table on top of the bed like that?"

I looked over at the furniture in question and shrugged in response.

"And is that my shift? Why is it hanging from the table leg?"

"That's my castle's flag."

"I see." She didn't say anything else, just moved slowly around the room silently taking note of my work.

"Do you like it? It's our very own castle."

Her mouth hung open for a minute before she said anything. "It's wonderful. Is it okay if I put everything back the way it's supposed to be, now?"

I frowned at her.

"I don't want to, but I don't want us to get in trouble with the inn."

"I guess. I don't want you to get in trouble either."

"Thanks, sweetie." She'd already started putting everything back before I'd answered.

"Did you get the job you wanted?" I jumped on the mattress she was trying to fix.

She grinned at me. "I did. I start tomorrow."

"We get to go see Arthur?" I asked, excited.

She shook her head. "I found someone willing to watch you for me. An old woman that lives near the temple. She takes care of all the children of the temple's servants. You'll probably get to play with all the little friends you made at the park today."

I glowered at her. "I want to see Arthur."

Her smile vanished. "I'm sorry, but it's just not safe for me to bring you inside. I'll find Arthur and tell him you miss him. I'm sure he'll come see you as soon as he can after that, okay?"

I found her answer both unsatisfactory and a little insulting, but I'd never really been one to argue with adults —too much—so I simply nodded. I made sure my expression was as forlorn as possible, though.

If she noticed, she pretended not to.

———

Arthur almost enjoys the time in his cell. It is small and dirty, but he has no cellmate, and as hard as the sleeping pallet is, it still allows him to stretch to his full length.

All the other cells in this section of the temple are empty, save one. Its occupant has been dragged away for their morning beating.

Arthur does not remember that ever being a part of the warden's duty, but the prisoner is an orc, and he supposes that even thirty years later the actions of Garack Bloodfist have left an unsatisfied anger in the guts of the paladins.

Down the hall a door opens and the sound of angry laughter and snide comments make their way to the bars of Arthur's cell.

He opens his eyes and, from his prone position, watches as the orc woman is dragged down the length of the corridor and thrown inside her open cell.

The bars are slammed shut and the warden throws one final insult at the orc. "Soon, tuskie, soon."

"Aw, but won't you miss our time together?" Her voice is rough, even for an orc. She sits up and shows the guard her tusks.

Arthur winces at the sight of them. They have been broken off almost at the gums. He is amazed that she can speak, let alone *smile* at the paladin.

The paladin lets out a low growl. He seems angry that the woman can move at all. Must not have much experience with orcs.

The warden reaches for a whip hanging at his belt. Arthur wonders how he will whip the woman through the bars. Maybe he actually has the guts to open the door now that she seems to have recovered.

The other knight, who had helped the warden drag her to her cell places a hand on his shoulder. "Come off it, we don't have time for you to play with her anymore today. Clay wants our report."

The warden spits on the floor of the orc's cell. The two turn to go, but the warden slows when he glances and sees Arthur watching them.

"Oh, don't you worry, *Sir Shield*. You'll get your turn soon enough." He laughs as he follows his companion.

"So, you're him, huh?" The orc woman has somehow already found her feet and is leaning against the bars of her cell, watching the idle Arthur.

He stares at her without saying anything. He knows he should have no animosity toward this woman. Even if she is an orc, as far as he knows she has never been a bandit, has never actually broken any law other than being born the wrong race, but he still can't help but feel a pang of hatred in the pit of his stomach.

She laughs harshly. "Fine, don't answer. You definitely must be a paladin of Saban if you're gonna glare at me like that." She turns away from him and sits down, back against the bars.

He closes his eyes and tries to sleep.

"They think we know each other, by the way."

He opens his eyes and looks across the hall again. She is staring at the grimy wall of her own cell.

"What do you mean?" he asks.

"They asked me about the girl. Apparently, all orcs know each other."

"What girl?"

"The Goretusk girl." She glances over her shoulder at him. "Are you really *the* Arthur Shield?"

He finds no reason to lie and nods.

She laughs again. "Then why the fuck are you traveling with an orc girl? Some real shit must have gone down for Arthur Shield to be protecting an orc. Not to mention a Goretusk."

She groans slightly as she pushes herself back to her feet. "Why you protecting an orc girl? Or are they mistaken? Gods know they like to make mistakes."

"That's none of your business."

She points to one of her broken tusks. "I'd say they went and made it my business."

He considers that. Part of him, and he is surprised to find it is the greater part, feels responsible for that. He sits and faces her. "Why are you here?"

She snorts. "I was working an escort job. Protecting a merchant caravan heading to the city. Patrol outside the city saw me and arrested me."

"For what crime?"

"Same crime they always get us for. Being an orc too close to Glanzend." She shrugs. "Mostly my fault, honestly. I should know better. Great Wood's about the only place this side of the Eastern Spine it's safe to be green."

"You have a license to work as a mercenary?"

She glares at him. "Of course I do. You think your brother's out there give a kobold turd about that?"

He sighs. "They should, but I see your point. A lot seems to have changed since I was here last."

She studies him in silence for a moment. The only sound her breath rattling through a broken nose. "You really are him, aren't you?" she asks at last.

"What possible reason could I have for lying about that?"

"I don't know. But they really don't want to believe you, do they?"

"No, they don't."

"At least they're not beating you, yet."

"I have a character witness arriving today. If he doesn't remember me, they'll probably start. Or just kill me outright."

"That second option might be better. No offense, but you don't look like you could hold up to too much."

"Why? Because I'm old."

"And human."

He grins humorlessly at her. "You'd probably be surprised."

"If you really are Arthur Shield, maybe. So, you never answered my question. Why you protecting an orc girl?"

"Half-orc," he clarifies. "And, honestly? I'm not completely sure myself. I keep telling myself it's because I made a promise that I would."

"Promise to who?"

"A murderer." The bitterness in his voice is as fresh as ever.

She stares blankly at him.

He wonders why he feels compelled to answer her questions. Could it be because she pretends to believe him? Or at least doesn't curse his every word?

"Have you ever learned something about yourself? Something that makes you second guess and doubt any and every choice you've made in your life?" he asks her.

"Can't say I have. But I'm a simple woman. Give me an axe to swing and something to swing at, and I'm usually pretty content."

He stands and approaches his own bars, mimicking her position, he leans on them. "I'm the same, actually. But do you ever second guess the reason you're swinging?"

"Not if the money's good." She grins at him, but he can see it in her eyes. Self-reflection.

"That's why I'm protecting the girl. There's no one else who will. And there's no one to hold me accountable if I don't. No one ordering it. No one but me." He has not realized it before he says it. But that is the reason. Whatever gods and demons exist can take Garack Bloodfist. Arthur doesn't care about that promise. He only cares that for the first time in his life he has made a decision on his own. No leash. No master pointing. Just him.

The orc woman nods along with his statement. "That's fair. Too bad they're gonna kill you, huh?"

He laughs at that. "I suppose so."

"Look, just on the off chance that they don't, you mind putting in a good word for me? I'm not really ready to die, just yet."

"I'll see what I can do."

"Thanks." She reaches through her bars, hand open.

Arthur reaches with his own hand and grasps hers. Her grip is weaker than he expected. The daily beating must have more an effect than she shows.

"Name's Ryta, by the way. Ryta Axejaw."

"Arthur Shield."

"Yeah, I know."

———

Hilda Farmer was a gentle old woman who, out of the kindness of her heart, looked after many of the children of the temple's staff. At least those that lived in the city instead of in the temple compound. She was kind and warm and smelled like fresh-baked cookies. I hated her immediately.

Hilda lived in a small brick house just a block away from the Temple of Saban. Compared to the rest of the city her neighborhood was quiet and subdued. It reminded me a little of the cul-de-sac my own family lived on. That familiarity only added to my distaste.

Not only was Hazel not allowing me to go with her inside the Temple, but she was also taking me away from the magic of Glanzend.

Hazel had walked me through the little gate in the stone wall up to the front door and introduced me to Hilda. I had returned the old woman's friendly greeting with a glowering scowl.

Hazel had apologized by explaining that I'd really wanted to go with her. Hilda had been *so* understanding. It had made me even angrier.

I only offered a token resistance to the woman leading me inside. She sat me on an overstuffed armchair and gave me a fresh cookie almost as big as my head. That explained the smell.

I took a reluctant bite. It was good, but I couldn't let her know that. I waited until she turned around before I took another bite. I made sure it was a big one, just in case she turned around quicker than I expected.

As the morning progressed more and more children arrived. It was almost enough to shake me from my silent anger at Hazel and Hilda. Among the group was a familiar face. The blond guard who had left me responsible for protecting the playground's castle. I decided that he was cute. His long blond hair looked better when it was being tossed by the wind, but I liked it inside, too.

I carefully climbed down from the chair Hilda had put me in and joined the group of children.

"Hi," I said to the boy.

He spared a glance from the platoon of tin soldiers he was arranging on the floor. "Hi."

"I'm Miki."

"Ok," he exclaimed as he shifted a few men in his army.

"What's your name?"

"Dederick." He didn't even glance up at me as he said it.

I narrowed my eyes at him. I was not in the mood for these games. He should just accept and return my admiration. Mom was right. Boys were the worst.

I sighed and stalked away. I decided, now that I was here, I might as well make use of the wooden crate of old toys.

I passed several other children who had already claimed their property. Girls with ugly dolls, boys with wooden horses and other strange creatures I didn't recognize. There were a few of the children who were staring across the room, eyes full of jealousy, at Dederick and his platoon of tiny men.

I got to the crate to find that it had basically been picked clean. All that was left in the bottom was a deck of cards held together by a piece of string. I picked it up and studied it. I didn't recognize the symbols on the cards, but as I untied the string and shuffled through the deck I decided it was basically the same as the cards I'd used to play games with my grandmother when she was alive. The old orc woman had loved card games. She'd even taught me one I could play alone.

I took my prize and found a quiet corner in the room. I

shuffled the cards the way my grandmother had taught me and began to prepare the game.

The room grew louder with the sound of laughter and arguing. No one ever claimed a houseful of children would be quiet. But, despite the noise, all I heard was the slapping of my cards on the wooden floor.

"What're you doing?" A voice interrupted my game.

I look up, irritated at the distraction. "Trying to play a game," I told the jerk.

My angry scowl faded when I recognized the speaker as Dederick. He stood over me with an armful of tin men. He and his soldiers studied me intently.

"What kind of game can you play by yourself?" he asked, seemingly unaware of the fact that he hadn't allowed anyone else to join he and his soldiers.

"Want me to show you?" I offered.

"Okay." He knelt, carefully arranging his army on the ground next to the cards before giving me his full attention.

I gathered up the cards and reshuffled them. His eyes opened in surprise at my ability to control the cards so well. His eyes were a nice blue. Like the sky.

"First you have to set up all the different piles." I demonstrated by slowly placing the cards on the ground.

"Dederick!" Another boy rushed across the room. "Are you done playing with the soldiers now?"

Dederick didn't look up from the cards, just shook his head.

"But you're not even using them," the boy whined.

"They're mine." Dederick's tone was so matter of fact that the other boy seemed to second guess himself.

"Nuh-uh, they're Granny Farmer's. They're for everybody."

Dederick rose and faced the boy. "They're mine." He sounded angry now.

"But you always play with them. I want a turn."

Dederick balled his hand into a fist. "No."

"But I—"

The whining was interrupted by a tiny fist connecting with his tiny stomach. The boy let out a surprised gasp. Clutching his injury, he turned and ran, wailing the whole way.

Dederick nodded, proud of his accomplishment, then sat back down. He stared at the cards patiently until I started setting up the game again.

"Aren't you going to get in trouble?" I asked.

He shrugged. "Probably. Granny Farmer doesn't like fighting."

He seemed so unconcerned. I grinned at him. I remembered my tusks and closed my mouth before he looked up. I did not want this boy to be afraid of me.

"Okay, now that the cards are all set up, you start by flipping this one over."

He watched me play until Hilda came over and dragged him away. She took the tin soldiers away and he screamed at her. He didn't cry, which I thought was very brave of him.

———

As has become custom, Arthur's wake-up call is a rude one. He is pulled from his sleep as the bucket of water is emptied over his head.

The cell is already cold—Glanzend is closer to Winter than Summer—and the water is enough to make the old man shiver uncontrollably.

"Time to get up, *Sir* Shield." The warden sneers down

at him. "Roderick wants to get an early start today. He's hoping we can prove you guilty before breakfast."

Arthur ignores the man as he rises. He attempts to dry himself with the thin blanket he's been provided but the warden knocks it out of his hands.

"Come on, old man." He prods Arthur with the short spear he carries.

Arthur can feel the blade as it breaks his skin. He keeps his face calm as he allows himself to be herded out of his cell.

"Good luck." Ryta salutes Arthur from her sleeping pallet.

Arthur acknowledges her with a nod.

"Oh, made friends with the orc, huh?" the warden says. "That settles it for me. No way you're Arthur Shield. He'd never make nice with the tuskies."

"I only ever had issue with orcs that broke the law." Arthur knows he shouldn't say anything, but he feels he must.

"Did I say you could talk?" The spear is jammed harder into Arthur's back.

The old knight jerks from the pain and his chains rattle loudly.

It would be so easy, he thinks. He could snap this weasel of a man's neck without even trying.

He shakes the thought from his mind. He turned himself in. He expected treatment like this. Does he deserve any better? Besides, what good would killing this man do? It certainly wouldn't help his case.

They climb the stairs from the cells and out the door into the morning air. The cold, late-autumn wind cuts through Arthur's wet clothing with more force than even the warden's spear had.

He clenches his jaw to keep from making a sound. He can't help the shaking, however. It grows more severe and his chains grow louder.

The warden laughs loudly to himself at the sight of Arthur's discomfort.

Luckily, the judgement hall is not far from the cells, and soon Arthur is escorted through a large set of wooden doors and into the well-warmed chamber.

If it were possible, the hall holds even more paladins than it has on any of the previous days of Arthur's trial. Many of the new faces are more aged than the knights who have previously gathered to watch the questioning.

Arthur is disappointed to realize that he still does not recognize any of them. He is not surprised by this. A lot can change in thirty years. He just wishes that less had changed.

He doesn't need the warden's instructions to step to the middle of the chamber, the man gives them regardless. Once Arthur is standing in the center of the room, the warden locks the chains to a loop in the floor.

Arthur instinctively tests the limit of his bonds. Just as with every time before, his range of motion is almost nonexistent. Both the manacles around his wrists and ankles are locked down tightly. Only his head is allowed free movement.

Once he is convinced that he is secured just as he always is, he turns his attention to the front of the room where Roderick Clay stands behind the pulpit.

Clay offers Arthur the same empty stare that he always does.

Arthur returns the stare for a moment before he realizes there is another man seated behind Clay.

He almost doesn't recognize the man. Victor Kraken has aged. The thirty years show on his face more clearly than

Arthur would have thought possible for a man who had once been as vibrant and alive as Victor.

His chin is weak and shakes along with the rest of the man. What hair is left on his head is a brittle white. His eyes are a milky shade of blue, seemingly unable to focus.

Arthur fears for a moment that the man has lost his sight in the years since they've seen each other. That fear vanishes when the old man looks at Arthur. His eyes narrow in an attempt to bring the chained man into focus.

Victor rises from his seat with the help of a sturdy staff. The staff clicks on the stone floor as the old man makes his way past Clay and toward Arthur.

"Sir Kraken, I am not sure that is wise. Witnesses tell us this man is dangerous."

"Of course he's dangerous." Victor's voice is surprisingly strong, despite his appearance. "If he is who I think he is, you're all lucky he hasn't fought back and killed you already."

The ever-present chatter of the gathered crowd falls silent at that announcement.

The warden steps in front of Victor, attempting to stop him from getting closer. The old man's staff cracks across the guard's face and he steps aside, eyes wide in surprise.

Victor stops, just inches from Arthur, and stares up at him. Arthur remembers when he had to stare up to meet the man's eyes, but now he is old and stooped.

"Is that really you, Arthur?" His watery eyes glisten with the promise of more tears.

Arthur's own throat tightens at the sudden rush of emotions. "Master Kraken."

Victor reaches out and runs a hand over Arthur's face. "When was the last time you shaved, Shield? And how do you look so young? You should be nearing your seventieth year, now. Always were lucky, weren't you?"

Arthur laughs. He wishes he could take the old man's hand, but he can't, the chains prevent it. "I wouldn't say lucky, Master Kraken. And it's a long story, but I still rest comfortably in my sixties."

Victor cocks his head in confusion. "But were you not past forty when you entered the wood to eliminate Bloodfist and his band?"

"Like I said, Master, it's a long story."

"I see. But it is truly you, isn't it?"

"It is me, Victor."

"Then I am sorry for the reception your homecoming earned, old friend."

Victor turns and glares at Roderick Clay more fiercely than his frail form should allow. "How dare you, Roderick. This is Arthur Shield, First Knight of Saban. He is owed all the respect you have to offer. All of you should be ashamed." He addresses the room, "This man has done more for this order than you could ever know. He traveled worlds on the order of our god, and you reward his return by chaining him and denying him even the basest hospitality. I demand you release him this instant."

"Is he truly Arthur Shield, Sir Kraken?" Clay asks, unaffected by the verbal assault.

"Of course he is."

"Very well. Then Sir Shield is found innocent of the crime of impersonating a paladin. Now his trial may begin in earnest."

"Trial?" Victor demands.

"Of course. He is still to be tried for the crimes of blasphemy and defamation."

"Blasphemy?" Victor turns to Arthur. "What have you done?"

"Spoken the truth, Master," Arthur answers.

Victor takes a moment to consider, then nods his understanding. "After ten years you might have expected the order to crumble. Through our stubbornness it has remained." His voice drops to a whisper that Arthur struggles to hear. "Through our deceit and pride it remains. Whether for good or ill, I still haven't decided."

"I knew it." Arthur shakes his head in frustration. "I knew it," he says louder to the room. "Why? Why can you not just accept the truth?"

Victor places a calming hand on Arthur's shoulder. His voice is still too low for the rest of the room to hear. "Don't blame them, Arthur. We were all scared. For the good of the nation many thought it best to continue as though nothing were wrong. For others, the loss of our status seemed too cruel a fate on top of our loss. The order in the capital is adamant that the truth not come out."

"And you?" Arthur demands, his anger shifting from the gathered knights to the old man.

Victor closes his eyes and sighs. "I am too old to make any changes."

"Coward." Arthur returns his attention to the rest of the room. "You are all cowards. Saban would be disgusted if he could see you now."

"Someone remove Sir Kraken from the room." Clay's voice cuts through Arthur's angry shout.

Several knights rise and cross to Victor. The warden steps aside, still in shock from the blow the old man had dealt him.

The men place respectful hands on Victor and gently turn him away. He makes as though to argue but stops after glancing up at Arthur's angry face. He allows himself to be led away from the prisoner and out of the room.

"I would ask that everyone leave." Clay meets the eyes of the gathered crowd.

There are angry murmurs, but everyone does as they are told and leave. The warden remains at his post until Clay clears his throat and glares at the man. The warden drops his head and leaves with the rest.

Once the room is cleared only Clay and Arthur remain.

No, Arthur realizes. There is one more person in the room. A young man, perhaps in his twenties, possibly thirties, stands near the door. He is not dressed in the militaristic uniforms of the order, rather a long robe of deep blue. Clay seems fine with the man's presence.

"Ready to confess?" Arthur says. "Now that we are alone?"

"I don't need to confess anything to you." Clay turns from Arthur to speak to the young man. "Now that we know, what do you think, Adrian?"

The young man, Adrian, pushes himself off the wall and approaches. He taps his chin thoughtfully as he walks around Arthur.

"There is still a residue of power in him. I can feel that."

"Will it be enough?"

"Perhaps. We still have the backup plan. If nothing else this should make the requirements for that contingency less severe."

"What are you talking about?" Arthur demands.

Clay considers him again. "Tell me, Arthur, how did Saban die?"

Arthur gapes at the question. "So, you admit it? You admit he's dead?"

"Of course. No knight that was in the order ten years

ago can deny it. We all felt our connection sever. The new paladins don't know. Some suspect, but none of us would dare destroy their faith."

"Why? Why pretend? Saban was the god of Justice. Pretending he still lives does nothing to further his cause. You can still fight for that. You can still uphold the laws of the world without him."

"I've heard this argument before, Shield. Victor made the same case ten years ago; that Saban has already taught us everything we need to be soldiers for justice."

"So why deny his death?"

"Because without Saban we are not paladins. We have no real power. It was the world's fear of him that made us what we are."

"You can't honestly believe that."

"You can't honestly deny it!" Clay throws the argument back at him. "Your name is no more than a scary story told to children at night. Did you know that? *Oh, don't steal, kids, or Arthur Shield will come find you.*" He smirks at Arthur. "I was told those same stories. Of course, it was different when everyone thought you were still alive. You were painted as an honorable attack dog. Now that most of the world thinks you're dead, well, they're not too worried about you hearing what they have to say. The real sad part is that most of the stories are probably true, aren't they?"

"What's your point?" Arthur has always taken the weight his name carries for granted, but hearing this, even always suspecting it, hurts.

"That the stories are going away. When they stop entirely we will be nothing more but a jumped-up police force that no one respects. We need that respect if we ever wish to accomplish the goal Saban set for us."

"What goal?"

"A world with no crime or injustice."

"And denying his death helps with that, how?"

"Let me answer that one, Roderick." Adrian steps in front of Arthur. "You see, Sir Shield, if the world thinks Saban is dead, they might be a little surprised when he comes back."

"What?"

"Sure, it might be normal for a god to rise from the dead, but it's simpler if we don't even have to tell that story. If he's just always been here, watching over everyone. Watching as they commit countless crimes against him. His watching also ensures his inevitable Justice against the sinners makes a whole lot more sense, too."

———

The sun was setting when Hazel returned to take me home. Many of the other children had already been picked up by their parents.

I'd learned from talking to some of the other kids that they were all the children of single mothers. Apparently, there was a war going on far to the south and many men had enlisted in the military and never came home. A lot of the boys had bragged that when they grew up they were going to join, too, just like their fathers. Dederick had refused to comment when he'd been asked. He just wanted to be a knight of Saban.

"How did you like it?" Hazel asked me as we walked down the dark street back toward the inn.

We'd got rooms at a new inn that morning. A cheaper one, Hazel had said. She hadn't explicitly said anything to me, but I'd overheard in her monologue to herself that she was worried someone might be looking for us.

"It was okay," I answered.

"Make any friends?"

I shook my head. I had, but I thought if Hazel thought I was miserable she might decide to take me with her into the temple compound. "Did you find Arthur?"

She didn't answer right away. "I think so. He was arrested."

I stopped and stared up at Hazel. She squeezed my hand reassuringly. "He's okay. I think. Now come on, it's cold. There's probably some warm food waiting for us back at the inn."

The prospect of food convinced me to start walking again. I didn't forget the conversation, though. "What happened to Arthur?"

"He was arrested because no one believed he really was who he said he was."

"They thought he lied?"

"Uh huh. But I heard that he was able to prove it today."

"So, they're gonna let him go now? We can see him again?"

She didn't answer for longer than I liked, and I repeated the questions.

"I don't think they're going to let him go, Miki."

"Why not?" I demanded.

She took her time answering again. "Apparently the other knights are mad at him."

"Why? He hasn't done anything wrong. Has he?"

I'd asked Dederick about the knights and he'd been more than happy to tell me about how noble and good they were. How they upheld the law and defended those who couldn't protect themselves. The image he'd painted for me didn't mesh with what Hazel was saying. Sure, Arthur could be a little grumpy, but my grandmother had been the same way, and she'd been a good person. And all Arthur had ever done for as long as I'd known him was protect me. The first time I'd ever seen him he'd saved me from a monster. Then he'd saved me from the angry elf and her friends. And there had been the scary old lady on the cart. There was no way he was a bad guy after all that.

"I don't know, sweetie," Hazel answered after another long silence. "I just don't know."

A FAMILIAR VOICE

One Year Ago
New York, NY

"So, remind me again what the point of this is?" Melody asks.

Arthur doesn't answer, just swings the wooden sparing sword and strikes her helmeted head.

"Fuck! Come on, I was asking a question!"

"No questions when fighting."

"Bullshit! This isn't a fight! You're supposed to be training me."

"Exactly." He swings the sword again but this time she raises her own, clumsily, and blocks.

She growls at him and swings her sword. The attack is pathetic, but it's followed by a succession of blows, all just as weak and inefficient, but there are enough of them that Arthur feels like he's done his job properly.

He flicks his own sword and hers leaves her hand. "Better."

"Better?" She stares at him in surprise. "You just," she flicks her hand, mimicking his move. "How is that better?"

"Just trust me."

"Whatever. Can we take a break now?"

He nods and she flops to the ground with a weary groan.

"You can ask your questions now." He sits down in front of her, legs crossed with sword resting in his lap.

"You really were a knight, weren't you?"

"Were?"

"Well, I mean, how long have you been here?"

"Too long."

"And you had magic?"

"It wasn't mine. It belonged to my god."

"Right. I get that. I think I read something about it in one of the coven's grimoires. It's like a pact or something, right?"

Arthur nods. "Close enough."

"Do you miss it?"

"Every day."

"Is that why you're always praying?"

"If I don't search for Him how can I expect Him to do the same?"

"But he's on another world?" She sits up straighter with this question. "Isn't that what you said?"

"Yes. I'm from a world known as Domhan."

"That's so cool. Like a reverse Isekai."

"What?"

"Nothing. Anyway, back to my *first* question: What's the point of this?" She waves toward her sword where it lies across the padded training room. "I'm a witch. I can just use magic whenever the company decides I'm ready to go out into the field."

Arthur nods. "True. Your magic is a very effective weapon. But what happens when you can't use it?"

She snorts. "What are the chances of that?"

"Very good, actually."

She looks concerned. "Really?"

"Look at me. My power is gone."

"You know, none of the others even believe you had powers."

"Do you agree with them?"

She shakes her head. "No. I think I can actually sense it."

He blinks in surprise. "Really?"

"I think? I'm not really sure. But there is... *something* there. I can't really describe it."

"I see."

"But my power doesn't come from a pact with anything. It's just mine. How could I lose it?"

"What happens if you're up against a more powerful witch? One with the ability to negate your spells?"

"Been there, done that."

He shakes his head. "No. You've told me how you managed eliminating your old coven. It took you weeks of preparation. And you personally knew every one of those women."

She looks down, her face suddenly paler than usual.

"A time might come when you have to face another magic user unprepared. One stronger than you. In my experience, the best way to deal with a powerful witch or wizard is to just stick a sword in their gut before they can prepare any spells."

"How much experience do you have with that?"

"More than you'd believe."

"Could you beat me?" she asks.

He glances over at her sword.

She laughs. "I meant if I was using magic."

"That depends. Have you prepared any spells against me?"

She suddenly looks ashamed.

He smiles at her. "Don't worry, Melody. If I have any say in the matter, when you attempt your escape, I won't be anywhere around."

"I don't know if I want to escape."

"But you're prepared for it?"

She nods.

"Me too."

"Really?"

"Yes. When Saban finds me, I will have to leave."

"Why don't you try to leave now?"

"I'm trapped here. My own strength cannot break the spell that binds me to Leanora."

"I might be able to help with that…"

He considers that but shakes his head.

"The consequences would be more severe than you'd deserve. I shall wait until Saban finds me. You just make sure you're not around then, okay?"

"Don't want to hurt your favorite student?" she grins up at him.

"I don't want her to hurt me." He stands up and points to her weapon. "Come, let's try this again."

———

Arthur is glad that his clothes have dried. The walk through the compound would have been completely unbearable if they hadn't. As it is, it's still very close. The cold chains hang heavier as he is led to the main stronghold of the temple.

It was one of the last places Arthur had seen before leaving to pursue Bloodfist. His heart beats faster as Roderick Clay and his wizard, Adrian Tinsmith, lead him deeper into the building.

Saban's palace. The levels below hold the temple's treasury, while above is Saban's throne room. The very room where Saban had ordered Arthur to pursue the orcs and goblins. Had ordered that their bandit army be wiped from the land.

Arthur had done what he always did. Obeyed. Drew his sword and charged at his lord's command.

Then he had fallen through a rip in the air. Twenty years of captivity followed. Many of those years were spent as a soldier for a different kind of master.

It was only recently that he'd realized nothing had actually changed for him.

"Where are we going?" he asks again.

"You'll see," Adrian replies. The young wizard seems excited.

"Are you going to explain what you meant about Saban returning?"

"Be quiet, old man." Clay steps in front of Arthur and raises a hand commanding him to stop.

Arthur does and waits as the knight unlocks a nondescript door.

Arthur recognizes this area of the palace as apartments. He himself had a suite of rooms several halls over.

Clay pushes the door open and indicates that Arthur should enter.

Once all three of them are inside Clay lights a lamp to reveal a modestly appointed sitting room.

Without a word Adrian approaches a bookshelf and pulls a volume from the meager collection. The book falls open and Adrian runs a slender finger along the lines, looking for a specific passage.

When he finds it he reads it aloud.

Arthur cannot understand the words. His head reverberates with the sound of them and he doubles over in pain.

Next to him, Roderick grimaces at the sound of the oily words.

Adrian closes the book with a snap and returns it to the shelf. As soon as it is back in its place the bookcase wavers, like a mirage in the desert air, then disappears.

Where it once stood is a dark doorway.

"Go," Clay nudges Arthur toward the door.

"Where does that lead?" Arthur demands.

"Seriously, Shield, why do you think I'm going to answer any of your questions?"

Arthur, again, considers just killing the pompous fool, but decides against it. He complies with the order and enters the doorway.

He finds a stairwell leading down and follows the stairs, their path winding around the strange circular tower behind the bookcase. Adrian and Roderick follow closely behind him.

Light filters up, growing brighter the lower they go. The steps end in a round room, well-lit by lanterns and a fire burning in a large hearth.

A long table takes up one side of the room, covered in glass bottles filled with bubbling liquid and strange smelling vapors.

But Arthur ignores that after he sees the middle of the

room. It looks like a well. A knee high circular wall of brick wide enough that Arthur could lie down inside it.

His stomach tightens, his old battle instinct warning him that a fight is close.

Held by the low wall is a roiling mass of black liquid. It looks like heated tar and smells like a day-old battlefield. Every hair on Arthur's body stands up as the air crackles from the dark magic that sustains the fluid.

"What is—" Arthur begins but is cut off by Adrian.

"Don't you recognize him?" The wizard laughs as he circles the vat of foulness.

"What?"

Adrian grins as he sits down on the low wall. "Maybe this will help." He rolls up a sleeve and reaches his hand inside.

There is a sickening popping sound as he breaks the surface. He fishes his hand around for a moment, tongue sticking out the corner of his mouth in concentration. "Ah, there it is." He pulls his hand out and proffers the item to Arthur.

Arthur steps back in disgust as the smell grows stronger. Then he takes another step back when he recognizes the item Adrian holds.

It is a helmet. Black as the tar it was pulled from. Its design is unlike any that exist on this world. As far as Arthur knows there is only one like it.

Stories are told about the set of armor it belongs to. Stories about how a god came to the world of Domhan wearing strange black armor. How he led an army of knights in battle and after their victory established an order dedicated to upholding the law of the land. Dedicated to peace and prosperity.

In Adrian's hand rests the helmet of Saban.

"What is going on here?" Arthur demands, barely holding back the bile that rises in his throat.

"I already told you." Adrian grins wider. "We're bringing back your god."

"That's right." Clay steps up and takes the helmet from Adrian. The black ichor runs down his gauntleted hands. "He will rise and give us back the power that was taken from us when you failed."

"This isn't right," Arthur insists.

"You can't say what is right." Clay rounds on him and brandishes the helmet. "The only being that can declare what is right and wrong is dead. But he's not going to stay dead." His voice is tinged with a desperate madness.

Arthur takes another step backward, but somehow Adrian is behind him. The wizard grasps Arthur's head in both hands and whispers something in his painful language.

Arthur falls to his knees and cries out in pain. The chains that have been his constant dressing for the past several days shatter and shards of ice cold metal cut streaks through his flesh.

"All we need to bring him back is a little power. Luckily, it seems like there's a fair amount left inside you."

Arthur stares up, unable to move as the intense pain spreads throughout his body. He has never felt pain this intense. Every muscle screams as though pushed beyond enduring, then pushed farther.

Adrian holds a hand to Roderick, who hands him the helmet. "I'm just going to take the little bit that Saban left you, Sir Shield, and give it back to him."

Holding the helmet in one hand, Adrian places his other on Arthur's chest. He begins to chant in his magical language again and Arthur screams louder.

A faint blue aura surrounds Arthur and, for a moment,

he feels powerful. Feels as he did when Saban lived and shared his strength. Then the glow moves. A channel forms between Arthur's chest and the helmet. The blue glow is siphoned away from Arthur and he feels himself growing weaker and weaker until, finally, the aura is gone completely.

From inside the helmet, two eyes shining with a brilliant blue light, open.

Arthur thinks he can almost hear a familiar voice before he passes out.

———

After two days of the same routine, I was getting bored. Every morning Hazel dropped me off at Hilda's small house. I made my way to the toy box and claimed the deck of cards and played alone in the corner.

At least twice a day Dederick would come over and ask me to teach him how to play cards and I would. Our card lessons were the highlights of my day.

It was during his second visit to my corner that I asked the question. "Have you ever been inside the temple?"

He looked up from the card he had been about to place. "Huh?"

"The knights's temple."

"The temple of Saban?" he asked.

"Uh huh."

He looked around, as though to make sure none of the other kids could hear his answer. All the other boys were gathered around the squadron of tin soldiers that had once been Dederick's, and all of the girls didn't even glance in our corner. For some reason none of them seemed to like me and as a result my corner was a quarantine zone.

He looked back at me and grinned. "I was inside there once."

"Really?" I sat up and leaned over the cards to hear him better.

"Yeah." He nodded enthusiastically. "My mom took me in to see where she worked."

"They're allowed to do that?" I asked, suddenly irritated at Hazel for not even considering the option.

"Yeah. It's like a whole other city in there. No one even noticed me. I snuck away from my mom and went and watched the knights training."

"Whoa."

"Yeah. She was pretty mad when she found me, but it was worth it." He sat back and crossed his arms, a smug look on his face.

"Do you think I'd be able to get in there?"

"Why do you want to go in? Girls can't be knights."

"Really? That's dumb." I considered the unfairness of the statement for a moment, but then decided it didn't really matter. I didn't really want to be a knight. I didn't know what I wanted to be, but I was pretty sure I didn't want to be a member of a club that had been so mean to Arthur. "That's okay, I don't think I wanted to be one, anyway."

"Then why do you want to go in? Just to see stuff?"

"My friend is in there."

"You have a friend in the temple?" His eyes opened wide in sudden respectful awe.

I grinned. "Yup. His name's Arthur and he went to see the knights to see if they could help me get home to my family."

"I thought the pretty lady that brought you here was your mom?"

"You think Hazel's pretty?" I found myself suddenly jealous of the woman.

He shrugged. "I guess. Isn't she your mom?"

"No," I confessed. "She's my friend, just like Arthur. She got a job at the temple to see if she could find him."

"Well, it is pretty big, I bet it'd be hard to find anybody in there if you didn't know where to look."

"Do you know where to look?"

"I bet I could find him." He puffed his chest out, adding to his smug demeanor. I believed him completely.

"Where do you think I should look when I get in there? Or do you want to come with and help me?"

His confident expression wavered. "Mom says I can't go back since I ran away from her last time."

"Oh. So where should I look?"

"Um..." He looked back down at the cards and flipped a few over while he thought of a response. "Maybe by the big building at the middle?" He met my gaze again.

He didn't seem as sure of himself as he had for the first part of my questioning, but I figured it was worth investigating.

I considered it for a while, then, decision made, I rose to my feet.

"Where you going?" he asked.

"I'm gonna go find Arthur."

"Now?" His voice carried the edge of a nervous shriek.

"Yup. Don't tell Hilda."

He sat frozen, a card in one hand and another half-flipped on the floor.

I passed the snack table—Hilda kept us stocked with cookies and other treats. All the cookies were gone, but there was a wealth of options as far as vegetables went.

I considered just passing by without taking anything,

but a short lifetime of watching movies and TV had taught me that I had to prepare for any mission, so I stuffed my pockets with carrot sticks before walking toward the front door.

I went slowly, making sure to watch out for Hilda. I spotted the old woman berating one of the boys—a young dwarf—for sticking a tin soldier up his nose.

When I was satisfied that the lecture would take a little while longer, I dug my cloak out of the pile and opened the front door.

I wasn't as silent as I could have been, and Hilda straightened. I slipped out and closed the door behind me.

I had no idea if she noticed, but I wasn't going to risk her catching me now.

From inside I heard one of the boys shout. "Granny Hilda! Dederick stole my toy!"

Dederick's angry response followed immediately. "Nu uh! It's my soldier!"

"Boys, calm down," Hilda's even voice raised just enough to be heard over the shouting.

I silently thanked Dederick for the unasked-for diversion as I rushed out the little fence and ran off down the street. I made sure that while I was in front of Hilda's home I ducked under the top of her short wall. Once I passed it there was a thick hedge—mostly just bare branches this time of year—that I was fairly certain covered my escape.

I wasn't one hundred percent sure of where I had to go, but luckily the walls of the temple cast a shadow over this part of the city and I was able to make my way toward them. Once I reached them I picked a direction that felt familiar and followed the wall until I found a door.

I was starting to regret my decision and thought sitting

down for a break might be a good idea, but the door encouraged me.

A man in armor—armor that somehow looked familiar, though I wasn't sure how—was talking to a woman pulling a handcart.

She was shouting at him as he flipped through a pile of paper. "I'm telling you the order was placed for today. Just look at that bill."

"I understand what you're saying, ma'am, but shouting isn't going to help me find it any sooner."

"This happens every time I make a delivery."

"Ma'am, I would really appreciate a little patience." He flipped another page. "Ah, found it." He gave her a look that reminded me of the few times my dad won a fight with my mom. The kind that says, "shut up and move on."

He walked to the back of the cart. "Let me just check everything."

"Are you serious?" the woman demanded.

"You deliver here all the time, ma'am, you should know our policy by now."

"Fine." She joined him at the back of the cart and the two of them bent down to compare the contents with the paper the man was holding.

I considered waiting to ask the man if he knew where I could find Hazel or, better yet, Arthur, but decided I wouldn't interrupt. He seemed busy. I was sure there'd be someone inside I could ask. I walked past the cart and through the open door.

The door led to a large courtyard. It reminded me a little of the cart station we'd entered the city through. There were carts lined up under a lean-to next to what I assumed was a stable. The sound of a horse whinny confirmed my suspicions.

Instead of a stone wall surrounding the area, though, it was a simple wooden fence. I didn't bother looking for a gate, and instead just climbed under the lowest of the thin logs that made up the fence.

Based on what Dederick had told me I'd expected the inside of the walls to be full of life and activity. It wasn't exactly dead, but it was nothing like the picture he'd painted for me.

Here and there, I spotted a group of men walking between buildings. None of them were wearing the armor of the man at the door, but almost all of them were wearing swords at their hips.

Along with the men, I spotted a lot of women. They were all dressed in the same uniform Hazel had been wearing the last few days. Simple brown dresses with the symbol I'd been told represented Saban stitched on the right breast. They all carried buckets or mops or bundles of firewood.

I studied their faces, hoping I might spot Hazel. If I found her then she and I could work together to find Arthur. Unfortunately, none of them were her.

I started to feel a little self-conscious and questioned whether I'd made the right decision. I was saved from having to make any sort of judgement call on my own when a man spotted me.

He disengaged from the small group of knights and approached me. I remained in place and waited for him.

"What are you doing in here, child?" He squatted down to eye level and offered me a warm smile.

"I'm looking for my friends," I told him. I looked at the ground as I spoke, suddenly unable to muster any courage.

"Who are your friends? And who let you in?" He

glanced around, as though he might spot someone that fit either category.

"I came in through there." I pointed behind me at the now closed door in the courtyard. The guard and the woman with the cart were inside unpacking boxes near the stable.

"I see. Well, who was it you were looking for, then?" His eyes narrowed in irritation as he glared at the guard in the courtyard but returned to friendly when he looked back at me.

"My friend Hazel is a cleaning lady here."

"Hazel? Has she worked here long?"

I shook my head. "Just a few days."

"I see. Well, come with me and we'll see if we can find her for you."

He offered me his hand and I reluctantly took it.

He led me farther into the compound. A group of younger men shouted out to my guide. "Hey, Basil, who's your lady friend?"

He waved them away with an irritated snarl on his face, but he made sure to smile reassuringly down at me afterward.

"What was your name, child?"

"Miki," I answered without thinking.

"That sounds familiar for some reason. And you're looking for a Hazel, right?"

I nodded again. "And my friend Arthur. Do you know where he is?"

"Arthur?" He stopped walking and looked down at me. His hand tightened unexpectedly.

"Ow," I said, and he released me quickly.

"Sorry. But who was your other friend?"

"Arthur Shield."

His eyes opened wide in recognition and before I could react he'd stepped forward and scooped me up into his arms.

"Let me go!" I shouted against his tight grip.

He ignored my cry and began to run in another direction, still carrying me.

"I said let me go!" I was scared. All I could think about was all of Hazel's warnings to be careful. All the times she'd insisted it wasn't safe inside the temple.

I panicked and did the one thing I could think of to get him to let me go. I bit him.

My tusks aren't big, but they're sharp. There was a burst of wetness in my mouth that tasted like pennies and Basil screamed in pained surprise.

I hit the ground running.

He shouted as I ran. "Someone stop the little bitch!"

I could sense the attention of everyone around shifting toward me, so I put my head down and ran as fast as my short legs allowed.

No one seemed in a hurry to chase me down at just that moment. I glanced over my shoulder to see Basil waving at me while a group of washer women and other knights circled around him, seemingly unaware of my retreat.

One of the knights followed Basil's wild gesturing and spotted me. He took off toward me and I turned back around and tried to run even faster.

I made it to the nearest building and had a moment of hope that I might actually escape, when a hand darted out of the doorway and pulled me inside.

I started to scream but the same hand covered my mouth.

Hazel dropped in front of me and held a finger to her lips, shushing me. "Don't make a sound." Without another word she picked me up and dumped me in a cart full of foul smelling fabric.

I was about to complain when she scooped up more of the fabric and shoveled it over me so I was completely buried.

I knew what this meant. I was hiding. I had to be quiet.

I started to sob. To counter my crying Hazel piled more dirty laundry over me.

"Where's the girl?" an angry voice demanded a moment later.

"Excuse me?" Hazel sounded genuinely surprised.

"The little girl that was running this way. I saw her come inside here."

"Oh, the little girl. No, she ran around the side. Who is she? Haven't seen any children in here before."

"Never you mind. Just keep your eyes open. If you see her again, make sure you stop her and bring her to the nearest paladin. Understand?"

"Of course, sir. I'll do my best."

"What's that sound?" the man asked.

"What sound, sir?"

"I thought I... Oh never mind. I don't have time for this." There was the sound of heavy footsteps retreating.

I started to dig my way to the surface but a wordless hiss from Hazel stopped me.

The cart began to move and I rode in silence. I was still crying, though I was fairly certain it wasn't loudly.

When the cart finally stopped I waited as Hazel unburied me.

Her face was a mask of rage. It was the angriest I had ever seen her. I began to cry harder, and I knew it wasn't quiet anymore.

"Be quiet," she hissed at me. "Do you know what they'll do if they find you?"

I sniffed and shook my head.

"They'll..." She stopped talking as she studied my face. Her expression softened and she sighed. "Never mind. Just be quiet, okay? I'm going to have to figure out how to get you out of here."

"I just wanted to help you find Arthur," I said, my voice wavering.

"Arthur? Oh, right." She looked worried.

"What?" I tried to sit up but the pile of dirty clothes shifted and I just fell back farther.

"What do I do?" She wasn't talking to me. I'd learned to recognize when she was having a one-sided conversation. "It's the last place I have to check. It has to be there, but I can't go now. Not with the girl here."

She let out another long sigh. "All right, sweetie, I need you to get back under the laundry and stay quiet. We're going to go find somewhere safe for you to stay, okay?"

I nodded and began to pull dirty clothing over myself.

Hazel continued to talk to herself as she began to push the cart again but I couldn't hear what she was saying.

I found a relatively clean piece of white fabric and used it to clean the blood that had started to dry around my mouth.

I'd managed to get my crying under control, but now I was shaking as I came down from the excitement.

I wanted to poke my head out of my hiding place and ask Hazel what we were going to do, but I didn't want to upset her any more.

Finally, the cart stopped moving and Hazel unburied me again.

"Okay, Miki. I need you to listen very carefully, okay?"

"Okay."

"This is the staff changing room. There shouldn't be anyone in here for a few hours, at least. So, I just want you to stay here and keep quiet. Can you do that for me?"

I looked around the small room to find rows of cubbies filled with folded clothing and lines of shoes along the floor.

"If you hear anyone coming I want you to hide in that closet, okay?" She pointed to a door.

I nodded my understanding.

"Okay." She picked me up out of the laundry cart and placed me on a long bench. "Now, please, *please* don't get into any more trouble."

———

One Year Ago
  Central Aanfang, Temple of Te Ora

Hazel has no more tears to cry. The child is only three hours dead but there are no more emotions left for the mother.

She sits and stares into space, not seeing the robed acolytes of Te Ora, Domhan's God of Life. She is oblivious to the murals of green forests and blue oceans, the creeping vines that climb the columns of the chapel. She ignores the questions posed by green clad priests and, if she does answer, her voice is hoarse from the week spent cursing and begging the gods.

Strong hands—familiar hands—guide her up from her seat and lead her through to the temple's sanctuary.

"You have to say goodbye," a distant voice tells her.

She shakes with newfound fury. Fury at the speaker—one she loves—and at the gods for doing this. "But she's gone!" Hazel screams in their faces. "She's gone! I can't say goodbye because she's already gone!"

The robed figures ignore her outburst and continue their seemingly pointless march around the large chamber.

Comforting hands are placed on her shoulders and encouraging words are shared. She sobs and covers her face, allowing herself to be led into the room she least wants to enter.

The stone table draped in deep blue is far too large for the wrapped bundle. Hazel's daughter was small for her age, but she appears even smaller resting on this surface.

"Is she..." She knows the answer but asks the question anyway. "Is she in there?"

An elderly priestess nods. "She is. We have performed our rights. Te Ora has released her from all obligations in this world."

Hazel chokes at the words.

The priestess continues, her tone too businesslike for Hazel to stomach. "A Charnel Priestess will be arriving shortly to shepherd the child."

Hazel does not respond, just stares, unblinking at the white and gold wrapped bundle on the table.

"Do you wish to carry her?" the priestess asks Hazel.

Hazel blinks in surprise. "May I?"

"Of course." The priestess motions to one of the other robed figures who gingerly lifts the bundle and carries it over to Hazel.

The weight is familiar but none of the warmth she remembers accompanies it.

"Please follow me," the priestess says, turning and walking back the way Hazel has just come.

Hazel follows, holding in her cries and fearing that the slight weight she carries might be too much.

The Charnel Priestess is already outside the temple, waiting and ready for her newest charge. The servant of the goddess death has not entered the Temple of Life. Theologians teach that Te Ora and Death—she needs no other name—are close. That they respect each other. But servants of one are not permitted entry into the other's holy places.

The woman is tall and slender, wearing a black robe lined with gold. Her skin appears untouched by the sun. Her eyes are lined with charcoal and her lips painted black.

She smiles sadly at the approaching party.

"You must be Hazel Midd." She offers Hazel a bow that would be too formal for a king. "I am here to escort your daughter to the land of rest."

She rises from her bow and holds her hands out, ready to accept the burden of the bundled child. Normally she would have a cart or a horse, but she does not need either to escort this soul.

Hazel hesitates, clutching the bundle more tightly to her chest.

A figure leans down and whispers into Hazel's ear. "Say goodbye, Hazel."

Hazel nods. She raises the bundle to her lips and kisses it once before passing the child to the priestess.

The woman accepts the bundle and presses her own black-painted lips to the same spot. "My mistress is kind. I know you do not believe that now, but remember, it is not Death that takes those we love. It is life. She just waits for each of us, offering rest at the end of our long—or short—roads."

Hazel watches from the temple entrance as the Charnel Priestess walks the path out of the temple grounds.

The woman has a long walk ahead of her. It is almost

five miles to the local cemetery where she and other priests will perform whatever rites Death requires before a body is placed in the ground.

Hazel watches the road long after her child and the priestess are gone from sight.

HARVEST

ARTHUR WAKES to a throbbing pain that covers his entire body. A groan escapes as he forces his body into a sitting position.

"Oh, still alive?"

The voice of Adrian Tinsmith surprises him and he responds with a wordless grunt.

"I was pretty sure I took everything." Adrian crouches down in front of him and studies him with excited eyes.

He reaches out to touch Arthur, but the old man throws a hand up and weakly attempts to push the other man away.

"I'm impressed." Adrian's tone is conversational as he rises and walks away, back toward the table of glass vials and tubes.

Arthur realizes he is still in the strange tower. His eyes dart to the vat of foul liquid.

There is less of it than he remembers. The surface has gone down slightly. He can now see a black breastplate just breaking the surface. It is Saban's. He thinks he can make out the outline of the helmet as well, the tar-like filth bubbling around it.

"It wasn't enough, if you were wondering." Adrian doesn't look at him as he speaks, just continues to pour the contents of different vials into others.

Arthur grunts another wordless question.

"Oh, the residual energy. Saban's leftovers, if you will." He turns to address Arthur directly. "You may not know this, but when a being like Saban shares its power with a mortal like you, they never take it all back. It's like... like when you drink a good thick beer. There's always the dregs. You know what I mean? Saban filled you up, you used what you could. When the source vanished—him dying, in this case—whatever wasn't taken back was still there. Just not usable. So, you actually had quite a bit for me to take. I managed to scoop it all out and give it back." He waves at the vat. "But you didn't have enough. Though, definitely more than any of the others I've harvested."

"Others?" Arthur manages to croak.

"Mm? Yeah. But, unfortunately, none of those old farts had enough in them. The energy had diffused a lot in the ten years since Saban died. But for you... well it was almost like it had just been there for a few months."

He considers Arthur again. "You did say you were on another plane, correct? A different world? I wonder if that had anything to do with it. Maybe some sort of time distillation? That can be a common occurrence in interplanar travel." He seems lost in thought for a moment, intrigued by this topic.

Arthur tries to rise but finds his legs are rubber.

"Oh, don't push yourself. Like I said, that procedure usually ends with the subject dying. It's a testament to your endurance that you're still able to move at all."

"How many have you killed?" Arthur's voice is growing stronger.

"I wouldn't say *killed*. A lot of them volunteered. Roderick's very good at selling this plan of ours."

"How many?" Arthur demands.

"Twenty or so. It'd be more, but we don't want *everybody* to know about what we're doing."

Arthur thinks of all his old friends and manages to find the strength to rise. He stumbles toward Adrian but loses his footing and falls. He manages to catch himself before his head hits the wall of Saban's pool.

"Impressive. Shame we can't find any more like you."

"Leave them alone."

"Who?"

"The others. My friends."

"Friends? You mean the men who condemned you to death for blasphemy? For telling the truth?"

Arthur winces at that. "Yes."

"Don't worry. I wouldn't be able to get enough power from them anyway." He walks the distance between the two of them and crouches again. With little effort, he helps Arthur back to a sitting position.

"Then you're abandoning this," he glares at the black-stained armor, "this blasphemy?"

"Oh, gods no!" Adrian laughs as he rises. "I've had a contingency plan in place since the start. Roderick just made me promise that I would only use it as a last resort."

"And this last resort?"

Adrian smiles down at him. "Well, I suppose I could introduce you."

"No need." The hair on Arthur's neck rise at the abrasive voice.

The old woman steps out of a shadow that Arthur knows had not been there an instant before.

"Sir Shield! So good to see you again," says Grannie Summer.

"Oh, you've met?" Adrian asks. He claps his hands together in excitement. "That's wonderful. Well, Madam Summer, did you want to explain to our friend how we're bringing his god back to life?"

The hag looks from Adrian to Arthur. "Did you really want to waste the time telling a dead man such a thing?"

Adrian shrugs. "I owe him a lot. He's brought us closer than we've been in years."

Arthur finds his voice. "You plan on using hag magic to resurrect Saban? How?"

"Well, we were about to explain that. Gods, does everyone get rude as they get older?" Adrian shakes his head in mock disgust.

"Sacrifice, good knight." Grannie Summer is suddenly at Arthur's side, kneeling down and caressing his cheek.

He tries to scramble away but his back hits the wall of the vile well.

"That's what makes a god, you know?" she continues, following him. She moves as though floating, raggedy dress billowing in an unfelt wind.

"Sacrifice? You're going to sacrifice me?" Arthur asks.

"Well... no. Not you. We've taken everything we need from you," she tells him. She smiles, her lips extending beyond the limits of her face. "You see, you know he's dead. Your faith died with him. What good would that do?"

"Then who? The rest of the order?"

"Why would we kill those who would serve him?" Adrian adds. "No, no, Sir Shield. There's a whole city out there. Did you know that almost seventy-five percent of the population of Glanzend still believes that Saban lives? Still prays to him to uphold the peace? I should know. I did a lot of unofficial polling." He laughs, as though that were funny.

Arthur's stomach turns to water.

"I think he understands, Adrian." Grannie Summer's smile spreads and her lips part to show teeth too sharp for her wrinkled face.

"Good. I didn't want to actually *say* it."

"You can't," Arthur says. "Saban would not want this."

"Fuck Saban," Adrian says with a laugh. "He's dead."

"But—"

"But we're trying to resurrect him? Yes. That's true. But it's the Saban that the order wants. Not the Saban you remember."

"That the order wants?" Arthur asks.

"You've been gone a long time, Arthur Shield. Things change. The knights of Saban want to be feared again. They want to rule. So that's what I—and Madam Summer, of course—are going to give them. A god that can be feared."

"And what do you get out of this?" he demands.

"Well, I just thought it'd be an interesting challenge," Adrian admits. "Haven't really had a decent project since I got kicked out of the old alma mater. Besides, Roderick has been paying me very well."

Arthur looks to the hag as she answers. "I get to murder and eat a city, good knight. What more could a hag like me want?"

"No." Arthur finds strength again and pushes himself to his feet. "I won't let you."

Adrian sighs. "Whatever you say." He reaches out and gently nudges Arthur with his finger tips.

The knight stumbles. The back of his legs hit the low wall and he trips.

The fall is short but feels long. The smell of death and

decay grows beyond his comprehension. He hits the breastplate. He had thought the surface had retreated enough to reveal the armor resting on the bottom of the pool, but that is not the case. The armor had been floating. As Arthur hits it, he and the armor sink.

He opens his mouth to scream and the vile, black substance rushes in.

———

I wasn't sure exactly how long Hazel had been gone, but I was almost positive it had been more than a few hours.

I'd exhausted all possible activities in the small changing room. I'd rifled through every cubby, tried on every pair of shoes, and eaten all the vegetables I'd brought with me from Hilda's house. Well, almost all of them. Some of them I'd stuck in the pockets of some of the cloaks and coats that hung by the entrance.

I was in the middle of my millionth lap around the room when I heard the door open. I froze in place. A wall of cubicles was between me and the door, but to get to the safety of the closet I would have to pass in view of whoever had just come inside.

I crept to the edge of my shelter and peered around.

A slender woman stood in the doorway, her long, pointed ears twitching irritably. It was the elf, Lara.

I quickly pulled back behind my cover. I tried to stop myself from shaking but failed.

Like any good elf, Lara made no noise as she rounded the corner. She grinned maliciously down at me. "I'd heard you were here, little orc." She held a small knife in one hand.

I slowly backed away, eyes wide in terror.

"Oh, don't worry, orc. I'll make it quick. Wouldn't want a child to suffer, even if you are a *Goretusk*." She said my family name as though it were the worst curse.

I wanted to say something, but I couldn't decide on the words. I'd never been so blatantly threatened before. I had a memory from what felt like years before of a group of armored men charging into a room and my father fighting them as mom and I ran. That had been scary, but I'd had so many people I knew around that I hadn't actually felt like I was in danger.

This was different. I knew I was going to die. I had no real comprehension of what that meant, but I knew I didn't want it to happen. So, I ran.

I wouldn't be able to outrun her—I'd challenged an elf to a race before—so I dove for the nearest cover I could find. I scrambled over the pile of clothes that filled the cubby and crawled my way through to the back.

I felt Lara's hand brush against my foot and I kicked out. I caught her hand between my foot and the rough wood of the cubby and ground my heel in.

She let out an angry snarl and threw her other hand in after me.

I slid farther in until I passed out the other side. Lara's hands flailed after me for a moment before she realized I was already out of the cubby and running for the door that she'd left open.

I heard cursing from behind me as Lara tried to pull herself back out through the cubby.

Once in the hallway, I panicked. I had no idea what lay in either direction but knew I couldn't take the time to deliberate.

I turned to the right and ran farther down the dimly lit hallway.

———

"Arthur?"

The voice rings familiar in Arthur's mind, but he doesn't have the clarity to recall why.

The old knight is drowning. He has long since sunk past the floating armor of Saban and continues to fall deeper into the impenetrable darkness of the black sludge.

He tries to swim, but the fluid offers no resistance. Motion has no effect on the foul-smelling substance. He simply sinks farther down into a pit that reeks more and more of death.

He is almost glad he cannot breathe because it means he can no longer smell.

"Arthur."

He throws his head to either side, trying to knock loose the strange voice.

"Why am I here, Arthur? Why are you here?"

He recognizes the voice now. It is Saban. He opens his mouth to reply and more tar pours inside. It coats his mouth, his throat.

He coughs, but the act only brings more of the substance inside.

"Arthur? Something is wrong, Arthur. Where is all my strength?"

A pocket of air opens around Arthur's head and he begins to vomit. Red is mixed with the black as it leaves his body. He is still sinking but the air follows him.

Saban's voice waits patiently while Arthur purges the poison in his system.

"Saban? My lord?" Arthur finally manages to gasp.

"Yes, Arthur."

"My lord, you are dead. You must know that. You must know that this," he waves about hopelessly in the pool of filth, "This is not you!"

The silence seems heavy. Arthur can sense the dead god contemplating.

"Saban is dead?"

"Yes!"

"But I am not."

"But, Lo—"

The air retreats and again the blackness forces its way inside his mouth.

"I know what I must do. I must return. I must save this world from itself."

Arthur allows more fluid down his throat as he screams silently into the dark.

"I sense it, Arthur. The sacrifices have begun. You shall add to the pile. Your strength shall become mine."

Arthur feels a sudden pain in his gut, as though a knife were stabbing out. His skin begins to burn and he convulses from the agony.

He continues to sink as the ghost of Saban begins its feast.

———

I somehow made it halfway down the hallway before I heard Lara shouting at me from the doorway of the changing room.

I thought I heard her footsteps coming after me and a tiny part of me that was aware enough to think about it was amazed that an elf would be so loud. It took a few steps before I realized it was actually the sound of bells.

I risked a glance over my shoulder to find Lara hadn't left the doorway. Her head was cocked to the side and one long ear stood up straight, listening to the bells.

She glanced down and we locked eyes. She shook her head and pushed off the wall toward me.

She started to close the gap much faster than I felt comfortable with, so I darted to the side toward an open door.

It was dark inside. Rather than rush straight into the darkness I hugged the wall next to the door. I hoped that Lara would just rush in blindly and I could sneak back out into the hallway behind her.

That plan changed when the square of light from the hallway was filled with her silhouette.

I instinctively inched away from the door and bumped into something. I felt the smooth wood with my hand and found that there was a space between whatever this furniture was and the wall. I managed to squeeze myself into the small opening as Lara's foot passed the threshold of the room.

I shimmied along the narrow passage until I hit the wall at the other end of the room. I found that the second wall continued around in that direction, as well, and I followed the path laid before me.

My eyes had started to adjust to the dark and I could just make out the woodgrain in front of me. It was rough and unfinished on this side and splinters had broken off on my cloak.

"I know you're in here, little orc." Lara's voice distracted me from my study of my hiding place. "I can *smell* you."

I started to panic. Did elves have noses that good? Or

was I just extra smelly today? I hadn't let Hazel give me a bath the night before. Maybe that was the cause?

"Ha!" I couldn't see her, but I pictured her lifting the lid off a barrel or something expecting to find me cowering inside.

She repeated the cry, this time in another part of the room. I hadn't even heard her move. I started to worry that she would figure out my hiding place before too long.

Her search was interrupted by the sound of heavy footfalls and a deep voice.

"What's going on here?"

"The girl," Lara answered. "She's in here."

"The Goretusk girl?"

"Yes."

"She doesn't matter right now."

"What are you talking about? Of course she does! Do you have any idea what the Goretusks did to my village?"

"Look, elf," the man spoke with a condescending tone, "Do you hear that bell? That's a call to arms. All the temple's paladins are being called to gather in the courtyard. I'm just here to grab a sword. Now just step aside."

"You won't help me find her?"

He sighed. "I think maybe you should just return to your rooms. Now might not be the best time for you to be walking around. Come on."

"Don't touch me!" There was the sound of flesh hitting flesh and I knew she must have slapped him.

The man laughed. "Never did like elves." There was a quiet rasping sound.

"Are you threatening me?"

"No threat. Tonight's just a night for killing. Might as well get started."

"With that little blade?"

"Well, I told you I was here for a sword, didn't I?"

"Like this one?" Something bumped against the other side of my hiding place and I shrunk back farther into the wall.

"Hey, put that do—" He didn't finish his sentence.

"No one tells me to return to my room." Something metallic hit the floor and rang out.

"Now, where could you be, Goretusk."

My wooden shield vibrated from a sudden impact and I let out a scared squeak.

Lara laughed and there was the sound of more metallic objects being knocked from the other side of my hiding place and hitting the ground. It sounded like she was climbing the wall and knocking pots and pans out of her way.

"There you are." I looked up to find her teeth glowing in the dark as she sneered down at me.

"No!" I shouted.

I tried to throw myself back against the wall again. When the wall prevented me moving farther away from her I threw my arms and legs up and pressed them against the wood in front of me, hoping to push myself back away from my pursuer.

I was surprised when the wooden wall shifted.

Almost as surprised as Lara. Her eyes opened wide as her perch began to tip backward.

I didn't think, just kept pushing.

Lara let go of the top of the wall and I heard her hit the ground, but I didn't stop.

More and more items from the other side of the wall were clattering against the ground now, wood and metal against stone. Then the entire wall fell.

It fell quickly enough that Lara only managed half a scream.

I didn't want to stick around to witness the aftermath of my lucky break. I jumped up on the collapsed wooden wall and ran across its surface toward the open door and my hoped-for freedom.

I skidded to a stop when a man in armor stepped into the doorway. He was flanked by more men dressed just like him. They all wore helmets with the visors up so I could see their expressions.

His cold eyes took in the mess of the room.

I glanced around. I could now make out that my hiding place had been a shelf holding weapons. Every wall of the room was home to identical shelves. Swords and spears and shields hung on display and ready for use.

A hand stuck out from underneath my hiding place and a puddle of glowing silver was slowly spreading past it. I quickly looked away.

I offered the knight an apologetic smile.

He reached for his belt and drew a long knife.

I couldn't hear the bells anymore as the man entered the room, but I could hear screaming.

POWER GIVEN AND POWER
TAKEN

Six Months Ago
   New York, NY

Arthur Shield is free. After almost twenty years of prayer his god, Saban, has found him. The power came rushing back, stronger than Arthur ever remembered it, though he suspects this is just a result of being without for so long.

He has fought his way out of the cell blocks and has climbed down an elevator shaft. He forces the door open several floors above the ground floor. He has been with the Dongli Conglomerate long enough to know that the lobby will be filled with security, and not just the kind that carry guns. Formidable warriors fill the ranks of the company, and Arthur does not relish facing so many of them all at once. Besides, despite himself, he has come to consider some of them friends. Even as a prisoner and an attack dog, he has learned to accept parts of this life.

But that's over now. He is free, his power has returned, and he can finally complete his mission.

"Freeze, Shield."

Arthur doesn't stop, but continues to walk toward the nearby window, ignoring the man.

A gun is fired. Arthur expected this and already has his protection up. A wall of blue light flares, catching the bullet.

"Melody, stop him!" The man shouts.

Arthur stops and turns, praying that he heard the man wrong. He hadn't.

Melody stands, half a pace behind the gun wielding man. Both are dressed in the company's official crisis response bullet-proof vests. The man wears his over a rumpled suit, and Melody over a black dress.

Arthur hasn't seen her in several months, and last he had heard she had been assigned to a team. If all accounts are true, she is an efficient fighter. Arthur believes it.

"Hello, Melody," he says.

"Hi, Arthur," she looks at her feet, uncharacteristically timid.

"I said stop him! Not talk to him!" her handler shouts.

"He stopped, didn't he?" she snaps.

"Tch, fine. Shield, surrender now and return to your cell."

"I can't do that." Arthur doesn't move, but he prepares every defensive spell he has. Melody is likely prepared. He knows she has countermeasures in place for any contingency, including fighting him. He just hopes he can get away without hurting her.

"So, you really do have powers, huh?" Melody says.

"They are Saban's powers, but he allows me to use them."

"Just like you said."

"I wouldn't lie to you."

She looks up at that, her eyes wide with some

unreadable emotion. "And now you're going to go kill the monsters, right? The ones who attacked your temple?"

"That is my mission, yes."

The handler looks back and forth as the two speak. "Hey, don't ignore me!"

They ignore him.

"Are you going to try and stop me?" Arthur asks the girl.

"Should I?"

"I'd prefer if you did not."

"Okay." From a bag hanging at her side she pulls out a small doll made from straw. In her other hand she holds a long needle. The needle is plunged into the dolls neck.

Arthur braces for the pain, but it doesn't come. Not for him.

The man in the suit drops his gun and throws both hands to his neck, trying to stop the sudden river of blood that pours down his side.

Melody steps around him toward Arthur. "Let me come with you. I can help."

Arthur considers her offer. He cares for this girl. He has never had children of his own, but he supposes he sees her as a daughter. It is that bond that forces him to shake his head. "No. You must stay here. The punishment for betraying the company can be severe. I am prepared for that for myself, but you are just a child."

"I am not!"

"I'm sorry, just compared to me."

"But, I've already betrayed the company." She waves toward her handler, who has dropped to the floor and stopped moving entirely.

"No, you haven't." Arthur gently pushes her aside and approaches the man.

He bends down and touches the body. He wills a small

flame to catch the man's clothing and it quickly spreads. Soon there is only a pile of ash.

"Only I have killed today."

"What should I do?"

"Tell them that I overpowered you."

"I meant, what do I do without you here?"

"Maybe I'll be back. Who knows?"

She drops her head again before rushing him and throwing her arms around him. "We'll meet again."

He can sense something from her, now. It mingles with the power of Saban that courses through his veins. She is still young and not yet in complete control of her power. He does not think that she gives this gift intentionally.

He supposes it would be considered dark magic, but it is Melody's, so he cannot be disgusted by it. Maybe it will give him an edge in the battles to come.

"Goodbye, Melody." He places a gentle, blood covered hand on her head.

"Bye, Arthur." She is crying.

He would never have expected tears from this girl, but there they are.

He removes her arms from around his waist and walks away. He does not look back, but he can feel her watching him.

———

The knife in Arthur's stomach twists again. Arthur knows what it is digging for. Whatever residue of Saban's power that still rests inside him is being hunted and devoured by the filthy tar.

If there was anything he could have done he is too weak now to attempt it.

The knife stops. It is as though it has hit a wall within Arthur. No, he realizes. Not a wall. There is a layer of armor within him. One he has known was there, but never been able to touch. It shields a small well of power.

A gift from a girl he loved like a daughter. A gift he cherished enough to hide away.

"Have you betrayed me, Knight?"

The voice is stronger now. Arthur has the sense of mind to realize this means that Adrian and Grannie Summer have likely begun the work of sacrifice.

"Have you taken strength from another?"

Saban is dead. Arthur thinks the thought as loudly as he can and his bottomless prison shivers at the words. *He is dead and you will never replace him.*

"I will be his better."

By killing?

"Their deaths shall save this world."

How is this justice?

"I am Justice."

No. You are a pile of filth.

The armor shifts inside him. His pain is still incredible, but he finds the strength to move. He reaches up. He has been falling for so long, but he must try. If Saban were still alive, surely, he would command Arthur to protect the people of the city?

Or maybe not. He wavers and begins to sink faster. Saban had once ordered the eradication of a world for its willingness to defend the orcs who had defiled his temple. Would he truly be against burning a city if it meant his life?

Arthur reaches higher, his arms shake from the effort. It doesn't matter what Saban would want. Saban is dead. What matters is what Arthur wants.

167

He thinks of Melody. She had murdered her teachers, her adopted family, to save her small town. Arthur will never be able to face her if he doesn't do the same. He suddenly wants to see her again.

And the woman. Hazel. The young witch that hates him so much. Why does he want to save her? He doesn't know why, but he does.

Then, there is the girl—Mikaia Goretusk. The granddaughter of one of Aanfang's most feared murderers and bandits. The little girl that trusts him explicitly. He finds, deep down, near the power Melody has given him, that he wants to protect that child more than anything.

Not for Saban or his killer, but for himself. For the sake of protecting.

Arthur's hand breaks the surface and he grabs the stone wall. He doesn't know how he has moved, but he knows better than to question. Melody has saved him. Now he must do the same for so many others.

He pulls himself free from the well and falls forward, a sliding, filthy mess. He lies on the floor and vomits. He fears it will never end. The tar is more red than black as it leaves him, but he forces himself to keep rejecting it.

He climbs to his knees, dry heaving.

"How dare you reject me?"

A sudden pressure exerts itself over Arthur and he is pushed down by the invisible force. He grunts with the effort of staying upright.

The small flame behind his internal armor flickers and Arthur recognizes the power that attacks him. It is dirty, polluted and wrong, but it is the same power that he commanded for all the years he served his god.

It was as much his power as it ever was Saban's.

So, he takes it back.

The armor protecting Melody's gift slides open and, like a pump primed, a torrent of power pours into Arthur. Strength fills the old knight and he rises to his feet. It is not the same as it was, but it burns within him, a familiar warmth.

"NO!"

"Don't worry, I'll be sure to give it all back to you when I'm done." He turns from the now writhing surface of the pool and walks up the stairs.

He is a short distance up when the bells become audible and he forces himself to run.

He can feel the weariness, the weakness, but it is underneath the sea of crashing power. He is outlined by a dark light. Where Saban's power had shined blue, this glows a dark purple, but it feels so similar.

It fills him like gas filling a balloon. And with the gas is the tiny flame gifted him by Melody. When he's ready he knows he can combine the two, but he must wait for that.

He bursts out the top of the stairs into the room from before. He studies the room quickly and finds that the bookshelf again covers the doorway down.

It doesn't matter. He leaves the room and rushes toward the sound of screaming and dying.

————

Hazel Midd has never been so scared in her entire life. She's so close. She knows that. There is only one building she had left to search. It is also the only building that none of the cleaning staff were permitted to enter.

"Should have checked there first, Hazel," she tells herself as she sneaks through the growing shadows of the courtyard.

The door is unguarded. At the sound of the bells every paladin and member of the temple's staff had rushed to whatever announcement the First Knight, Roderick Clay, had to make.

More than a few of the knights had been dressed in full armor and carried weapons. While that was not unheard of, Hazel had never seen so many at one time equipped for battle.

"Battle," she says under her breath as she descends the stairs into the small stone building. "Of course there's going to be a battle, because your day hasn't been shitty enough." She pauses and stares back up the stairs. "I hope Miki's okay."

She puts the girl back out of her mind for the time being. She has something more important on her mind right now. She feels bad for considering the child less important, but she knows her heart, and if she's right, then her heart is here.

"Oh, decide to take me with after all?" a familiar voice asks.

"Ryta?" Hazel asks.

"Hazel?" Ryta Axejaw moves the arm that was covering her face and sits up on her pallet. "Is that really you?"

"Oh, gods, Ryta!" Hazel rushes to the bars of the cell and reaches in toward the orc woman.

Ryta almost trips in her rush to cross the distance. She takes Hazel's hand in both of hers before reaching around the bars and pulling Hazel into an almost too strong hug.

"I knew it," Hazel is crying now, "I knew I'd find you. I knew you were still alive."

"You little idiot," Ryta says as she showers the top of Hazel's head with kisses. "What stupid reason could you have for sneaking in here?"

"Just you." Hazel manages a broken laugh through her tears.

Ryta smiles down at her love and Hazel's face pales. She reaches up and tenderly touches the broken tip of one of Ryta's tusks.

"What happened?"

"This? Psh, no big deal. They grow back."

"Who did this to you?" Hazel's voice is like iron.

"No one you need to worry about. If we see him, he's mine to deal with."

Hazel clenches her jaw but concedes. "Step back, I'm going to get you out of there."

"How are you planning on getting me out of the temple, though? Not that I want to downplay how fucking incredible you are in getting here, but, well..." She still steps back from the bars as Hazel pulls out her small wand.

"The paladins are distracted. They're up to something big out there." Hazel aims the bone white twig at the cell's lock.

"Yeah, I heard the bells. I wonder..."

"What?" Hazel looks up from her focus on the cell's door.

"Just made a friend down here. Just wondered if he was okay."

"Arthur?"

"You know him?"

Hazel nods. "Is he... is he okay?"

"No clue. Hang on... the knights were questioning me. Something about Arthur traveling with a half-orc girl and an unknown woman. That you?"

Hazel nods. "I think you'll like her. Oh shit, we should hurry, I left her alone."

The end of her wand flashes for a moment as Hazel

thinks the silent spell she's had prepared since she knew she would have to rescue Ryta.

"Where'd you leave her?"

"Staff changing room."

"Staff?"

"I'm a maid now." Hazel steps back as Ryta pushes the cell open.

Ryta says nothing, just scoops the small woman up off the ground and kisses her.

"Thank you," Hazel says.

"No, that was *me* thanking *you*. Now, any idea where I might be able to get myself a weapon or two?"

"There's an armory on the way."

"Perfect."

Objectively, Hazel knows that Ryta's smile—with the broken tusks and malicious gleam in her eyes—should be horrifying, but she just thinks it's beautiful.

———

The courtyard of the temple is in chaos. Arthur steps from the palace to find armored knights slaughtering their unarmored brothers and chasing down fleeing women in the uniforms of the cleaning staff.

Anger rises in his chest and the dim purple light around him flares brighter.

A paladin charges past Arthur, swinging a sword and cutting down an elderly woman. "For Saban!" He raises his gore-soaked blade and shakes it to the darkening sky.

He doesn't notice the glowing man that approaches him. Doesn't feel the blow that crushes his spine.

Arthur picks up the man's sword and marches farther into the courtyard.

"Do you hear me, knights of the dead god?" he shouts his question into the chaos of the slaughter.

Several armored men stop their work and turn to face him. In the quickly fading light of the dead day he can see the surprise on their faces.

Those not equipped for battle take the opportunity to flee.

Most of the knights ignore them. The glowing man holds their attention.

Arthur spares a glance for those fleeing and growls when a squadron of armored knights cuts off the retreat. The air fills with cries of "For Saban!" as the men and women are killed.

"Why?" Arthur demands.

"Who are you?" One of the knights shouts at him from across the courtyard.

Arthur raises a hand and studies it. He is still covered in the filth from the dead Saban's pit. The strange glow is sure to confuse them anyway.

"You're not Roderick's wizard. Are you with Summer?"

"You know of Adrian and the hag?" Arthur asks. The anger in his chest grows.

The wall of armored men stop behind the knight Arthur is questioning and give each other curious looks. More knights join them, all studying Arthur.

"Of course we do. It's working isn't it? When's Clay going to give us the power?"

"You get no power."

"What?" the knight scoffs. "Why not? We're getting ready to march on the city, we sure as the hells better get access to that after what we're doing tonight."

"No."

"What, you plan on keeping it all for yourself?" The

gathered knights laugh at that, as though all the death around them were just some social event.

"You misunderstand me." Arthur raises his sword.

The paladins recognize the aggression and raise their own weapons and shields.

"My name is Arthur Shield."

His name has the desired result. They visibly tense, some even inch away.

"Clay said he killed you..."

"He and his wizard and his hag tried. But here I am." He raises his voice so any knights that haven't joined their companions might hear. "My name is Arthur Shield. I have passed through the space between worlds. I have killed witches and wizards, orcs and goblins. I was the First Knight of the noble god Saban, leader of the order of Justice. I have climbed from a god's grave and stolen his power for myself. I am Arthur Shield and I am a killer. And tonight," he grasps his sword hilt with both hands and drops into a fighting stance, "Tonight, I kill the order of Saban."

The knights cannot let this declaration stand. They charge him. But they are just men. Arthur is more than that now. He is what he once was. A paladin of Saban. He was too late to save the dead, but he will mete out their justice.

These men are not paladins. They never truly were. They have weapons and armor and training. But Arthur has power.

That, and he's always been very good at killing.

The lead attacker lunges, sword tip aimed for Arthur's unarmored chest.

Arthur summons a shield. *Like riding a bike... is that what they would say on Earth?* The blade flicks to the side, sparks flying as it travels along the barrier.

Arthur flicks his sword up, using the first trick Saban

ever taught him with his power. "Swords can only get so sharp, Arthur. But my power can cut any steel."

The glowing blade parts the plate like paper and the man dies.

Arthur wraps a hand around the back of the dead man's head and hurls the body backward into the group of knights attempting to surprise him from behind. The group is scattered by the force of the blow and Arthur ignores them to carve a path through the men in front of him.

A man tries to throw Arthur down by pushing him with his large shield. Arthur returns the push with a ramming shoulder. The metal-rimmed wood splinters and the man flies back with a cry of surprise.

He casually reaches out and touches another man on the face. A portion of the purple glow leaves Arthur and enters the man. The fire catches almost immediately and the man screams. The smell of burning flesh drives other armored men away.

He turns and slashes down with the power-enhanced blade and rends arm from torso, the screech of tearing metal mixing with screams.

The more men he kills, the more arrive. Shouts and orders can be heard throughout the compound. More and more knights abandon their task of sacrifice to deal with the man who would stop their plans.

Underneath his mantle of power Arthur feels himself growing weaker. He knows that if it were not for this stolen strength he would be dead a dozen times over. But, he has the power while his enemies do not. Despite their training and obvious skill with sword and mace and shield, Arthur is stronger. He is also just better at the trade of death.

Arthur is graceless in his work. When he was young he had been praised for his skill. For his ability to flow from kill to kill like a dancer. As he grew older he'd realized that it was a waste of energy. He is economical now. He uses the minimal amount of energy required for each attack. A simple flick of the blade here, half a step in that direction, break an arm, crush a windpipe. He is a butcher at his block and the work is dull.

Any watching him would assume his heart is not in the killing, but they would be wrong. It is there. It is all that drives him forward. His anger, his rage, he takes it and channels it. Mixes it with the corrupted power that burns and cuts his enemies.

His face is a mask of calm that hides all he has harbored for twenty long years. He releases it now in rivers of blood and the screams of dying men.

He kills. He kills to protect those that Saban would sacrifice. He kills to save those that, despite them, he considers friends. He kills for himself because it is all he knows. It is the one thing he can do.

He kills until there is no one left to kill.

The courtyard is lit by strange purple flames that lick at plate armor like dry wood.

Arthur slumps to the ground, holding himself up with his sword. He has reached a limit he knew was coming. Even with the strength he'd taken from the pit his body is tired and old. Only so much can be done.

A lone figure considers him.

Adrian Tinsmith claps his hands appreciatively. "I'm impressed, Master Shield. How on Domhan did you manage to siphon so much power away from the fetus?"

"Wizard," Arthur snarls, pushing himself to his feet.

"Nuh uh. None of that now." Adrian speaks a word that feels like a punch to the face.

The purple glow around Arthur blinks out.

"I've returned that to its rightful owner. Severed the cord you tied yourself. I'm sure he's upset that you kept it for so long. Well done pulling that off, by the way. When I have more time, I'll have to study you. Find out how you did it. But, right now, I have much more important things to do."

Arthur finds he is weak again, his body feels every swing of the sword, every ungraceful dodge, every lucky blow landed. But, somehow, he manages to stay on his feet.

"Well, Master Shield, what now? You no longer have any magic, and I have all of mine. How do you plan on getting out of this one?" Adrian barely contains a laugh.

"Like this." Arthur's sword flies straight.

The young wizard doesn't have time to register its flight before it rips through the back of his robes. He paws uselessly at the coiled rope that spills from the wound for a moment before collapsing forward.

"Fucking wizards," Arthur growls to himself as he selects a relatively clean sword from those scattered about the courtyard.

Still a few loose ends to tie up. He picks a direction and marches off, hoping to find Roderick Clay.

———

Six Months Ago
Central Aanfang, Axejaw Farm

Time makes amazing medicine. The ache in Hazel's chest is lessened every day. The memory is still sharp and she does her best to grip it tightly by the blade, but the pain of loss subsides slowly.

Ryta Axejaw finds her by the fish pond.

Hazel sits on the blanket and stares at the surface of the water, the mirror surface only broken occasionally by fish just out of sight.

"What are you doing out here?" Ryta asks, taking a seat on the dirt next to Hazel.

Hazel smiles up at the orc woman. "Just enjoying the view. Is that a problem?"

Ryta returns the smile. "No. I was just hoping you might want to, I don't know, maybe see me off?"

"See you off?"

"Forget already? I'm leaving on that escort job today."

"Oh. Right. No, I do remember. Gods, I'm sorry, Ryta. I just didn't realize how late it was."

"That is the shittiest excuse I've ever heard. *Oh no, I forgot how to tell time!*"

"Shut up." Hazel tries to shove the large woman but Ryta doesn't budge.

Ryta laughs at the attempt as she rises. "Come on. I refuse to leave without a proper farewell."

"Proper farewell, huh?" Hazel spreads out across the blanket and covers her face with an arm. "But I'm just so tired. Maybe you could carry me?" She grins up at Ryta while peeking one eye from under her arm.

The orc bends down and lifts Hazel off the ground. The human woman lets out an impressive scream as she is thrown over Ryta's shoulder.

"Oh, shush. The neighbors'll think I'm abducting you." Ryta's breath doesn't catch as she begins the short hike back to their small home.

"What neighbors?" Hazel asks while pretending to beat her fists against Ryta's back.

"I dunno. The Grimhearts are only about seven miles east of us. They might be able to hear you?"

"I'd better shout louder then." Hazel cups her hands to her mouth. "Help! Someone save me! I'm being kidnapped by this dangerous orc woman! Help!"

"You do remember that all of our neighbors are orcs, right? If anything, they'd all just decide I had the right idea and march on the nearest village."

Hazel twists on her perch and tweaks Ryta's pointed ear.

"Ouch! What was that for?"

"Our neighbors are all lovely people who would never raid any village."

Ryta snorts. "Get Lucas Grimheart drunk sometime and ask him about his wild teenage years."

"And what about your wild teenage years?"

"Still living them, baby." Ryta clears the small grass-filled space that separates the woods from the small one room cottage. She bumps the door open with her hips and carries Hazel inside.

"Oh!" Hazel exclaims as Ryta drops her on the large, soft bed. "You weren't kidding about a proper farewell."

"You know it. You think I'd be able to get any sort of lucky in Glanzend with this face?" Ryta points at the two large tusks that protrude from her bottom lip.

Her exaggerated smile forces a muffled laugh from Hazel.

They take as much time as they are able.

"Be careful out there, okay?" Hazel says.

She is wrapped in a large quilt with her head resting on Ryta's shoulder as the orc ties her boots.

"I'm always careful."

"Bullshit."

Ryta laughs. "Look. It's Glanzend. You know I'm going to be careful."

"Have all your paperwork?"

"Yes." Ryta draws the word out and rolls her eyes in exasperation.

"Okay. When do you get back?"

"A couple weeks to get there, then the same back. Same as last time I made the trip. Promise not to leave me for that hussy down the road?"

"There's a hussy down the road? Which way? Just so I know which direction to avoid on my long, lonely walks."

"You are the worst." Ryta leans her head back and kisses Hazel one last time.

"I love you, too." Hazel's grin widens after the kiss.

Ryta rises and walks to the door. "I know." She offers her wife what she probably believes is a roguish grin and a wink before going outside.

The cart is already packed with the supplies Ryta will need for the journey to the small town where she is set to meet her client.

A simple job, she'd insisted. Just watching the backs of a couple fat merchants. She'll be home in no time.

She does not come home.

THE FINAL DEATH

HAZEL AND RYTA make their way through what was once the temple compound. Everywhere they look, they see death. Hazel recognizes many of the women she has come to know the past few days. Cleaning staff and even paladins lie dead around the temple grounds.

"They're not wearing their armor," Hazel notes.

"Hm," Ryta agrees. "The warden and his buddies were dressed for a fight last I saw them. Those wounds." Ryta clicks her tongue. "These people were running away. Either that or taken completely by surprise. Looks like we arrived in the middle of a good old-fashioned zealot civil war."

"But why? Why kill their brothers? The staff?"

"Don't ask me, babe. I never did understand most of you humans, anyway."

They both stop suddenly as they begin to cross a courtyard that connects to the building where Hazel left Miki.

The bodies here are different. Many are the unarmored knights and defenseless cleaning women, but even more are armored men.

Hazel marvels at a suit of plate armor that still burns with a strange purple fire. A charred skeleton rests on a bed of ashes inside.

Ryta whistles. "Fuck me sideways."

The two women tread carefully as they walk through the battlefield.

"Look at that. Cut straight through the plate! Gotta have a helluva good arm for that." Ryta bends over to study one of the corpses.

"And the fire," Hazel adds.

"Reminds me of the old stories they tell about the knights."

"Wasn't that blue fire?"

"Maybe the story got messed up before it reached our neighborhood?"

Their journey through the carnage is interrupted again when one of the bodies rises from the ground.

An old woman in a ragged, threadbare dress. Hazel realizes after a moment that the woman had not actually been on the ground like the rest of the bodies but had been hunched over something.

She feels bile rise when she recognizes that the something is a corpse. Gut split open and entrails scattered about it. Bites have been taken from the gray rope and the woman wipes a hand across a satisfied smile.

"Oh, I remember you," she says, pointing at Hazel. "You were the witch on the cart with the old knight."

The light is dim and Hazel can't quite make out the face of the woman. But the memory comes to her. "The hag."

"Oh, good, you remember me, too."

Ryta stiffens next to Hazel at the announcement of the woman's identity. "Are you serious?" she whispers out of the side of her mouth.

Hazel nods. She has already drawn the finger length piece of gnarled wood that is her wand. She doubts she's prepared enough spells to face a hag. She has only had so much time since the day in the cart. She's tried to refill the wand with as many attack spells as she could think of, but she doubts whether any of them will have much effect against a hag.

But she has Ryta. Everything will be fine as long as she has Ryta at her side.

"Oh, what a cute little wand." The hag has stepped through the shadows of the early night and is hovering over Hazel and Ryta, admiring the wand Hazel holds.

The two women jump back, each going a different direction.

"Ryta, find a weapon," Hazel orders without thinking.

Ryta is already bending down to pull a sword from a dead man's hand.

The hag smiles down at them. "Oh, goodie," she cackles with a malicious glee. "I haven't had too much fun tonight."

She waves a hand and the bodies scattered around the courtyard begin to jerk and move. They rise, shakily, to their feet and circle the two women.

"Motherfu—" Ryta starts before she is forced to swing her new sword to stop an attack.

The body crumbles easily under her blow, but there are so many of them. Hazel hopes Ryta can keep going.

Hazel empties several of her saved spells into the shambling mass of dead knights, and they fall to the ground like puppets with their strings cut.

The two fight, back to back. Hazel's wand lighting up with her wordless commands, and Ryta's sword cutting through the air and dead flesh.

Above them the hag floats, back and forth, cackling the

whole time. Her smile grows with every knight the two return to death.

Even as Ryta cuts down another dead man, the first she struck rises again.

The hag needs to be stopped. Short of completely destroying the corpses, there is no way to stop them from rising again and again. A headless corpse, with one arm only held in place by gnarled plate mail, shambles forward to be crushed under one of Ryta's powerful swings.

Hazel tries to keep track of how many spells she has used. She has no real way of sensing what is left in the wand, just her memory of what she charged it with and her best effort at paying attention now.

She does have one she knows she hasn't used yet. One she rarely prepares because it's not the most practical. Almost overkill, really. But the range is so incredibly limited.

She'd developed it years earlier and only used it once, before she'd met Ryta. It was to cast this spell that she had chosen the life of a witch.

Ryta had promised her once that if she said the word, that village would be burned to the ground. That had been the moment that Hazel knew she loved the orc woman.

That had been the night that Hazel's daughter had died of the fever. Ryta had never asked after the girl's father. But in her sorrow Hazel had shared the story. Ryta shared Hazel's grief at the infant's death, but she now shared Hazel's rage at her home.

And now, years later, the two women fight to protect each other; fighting dead men that won't die.

"Ryta?" Hazel asks in between spells.

"Hm?" Ryta can't spare the energy to speak.

"I'm going to need you to do something for me. Don't argue, just agree to it, okay?"

Ryta looks away from her current opponent and considers her wife. She nods before returning her full attention to her fight.

"Throw me at the hag." Hazel keeps her voice low. She has no idea how good the hag's hearing is.

"What?" Ryta almost misses her next swing.

"Do you have enough strength to do that?"

Ryta glanced up at the strange spectator.

"How close do you have to be?"

"Just closer than I am now."

"I hope you've kept up your diet."

In one motion, Ryta removes the head from a knight, continues the spin, drops her sword and lifts Hazel up in her arm.

She lets out her loudest berserker cry as she throws Hazel into the air.

Hazel balls her body up until she feels she is at the top of her arc, then she opens herself up horizontally, arms straight out in front.

A table's length, that is all she needs.

The hag blinks in surprise at the sight of the young witch at eye level with her, her smile doesn't waver as she watches the wand flash its brilliant white light.

Hazel's flight is spent and she begins to fall. The hag's dead body keeps pace with her, crumbling as they fall.

Ryta is underneath Hazel and catches her before she hits the cobbles.

"Ha! I love you, you crazy idiot!" Ryta lifts Hazel up and kisses her long and hard. Around them the bodies have stopped moving.

When Ryta finally puts Hazel down, the witch takes a moment to catch her breath.

The two of them check where Grannie Summer's body hit the ground and find a mound of black dirt writhing with worms. Bits of fabric poke up from the ground in the same flower pattern as the hag's dress.

———

I tried to back up, but the man was already in the room, his armor wrapped fist gripped my arm and he wrenched me from the ground.

I let out a cry of pain as he dangled me above the ground.

He pointed at me with his drawn knife and addressed the other knights. "This the girl Basil was complaining about earlier?"

The men all looked at each other and shrugged. "Maybe?" One of them said. "Maybe it's a cleaner's kid?"

The man looked at me, he almost looked sad as he studied me, but I didn't really care, it didn't change that he was hurting me.

"Let me go!" I swung my free hand wildly and he moved his knife out of the way.

"I guess it doesn't matter. Girl, do you believe in Saban?"

"Huh?" I stopped swinging and glared at him. "No. Put me down!"

"Think it really makes a difference if they believe or not, Clay?"

The man placed me down on the ground and I scurried to the corner farthest from the door.

186

"Probably not," the knight, Clay, answered. "You all get your weapons. The others have started already."

"Yessir." They streamed past him and selected weapons from one of the shelves that I hadn't tipped on top of an elf.

"I'll meet you all out there. I'll take care of this one."

Some of the men gave me sad looks but rushed out the room without comment.

After my experience with Lara, I was starting to understand why my parents had always insisted on not talking to strangers and I certainly didn't want this man to get any closer.

He took a step farther into the room and I spun to face the wall of weapons behind me. I grabbed the one closest to me. The long spear was heavy, but I gritted my teeth and swung it so the pointy end was aiming at the knight's armored chest.

He sighed heavily before swatting the tip of the spear aside with a casual wave of his hand. My whole body turned with the spear as I tried to keep my grip.

"For Saban," he said through gritted teeth as he aimed his dagger toward me.

"Clay!" A familiar voice shook the walls of the room.

Clay spun to face the newcomer and I saw him through the knight's legs.

Arthur Shield stood framed in the doorway of the armory. He was covered, head to foot, in a cracking and flaking black substance. It looked like he'd rolled around in a puddle of mud before coming here.

"Arthur!" I dropped my spear and jumped up and down in excitement at the sight of my friend.

"Shield?" Clay asked the man. "But how?"

"Your wizard's dead, Roderick." Arthur stepped inside the room and aimed a red-streaked sword at the knight. He glanced down at me. "Don't move, Miki. And maybe close your eyes?"

As he spoke to me, Roderick Clay jumped forward. He jabbed his dagger toward Arthur without any warning.

But Arthur apparently heard or saw the attack coming because he simply turned his body and allowed the stab to go past him.

Arthur let out a grunt of exertion as he brought his sword down into Clay's arm. There was the loud sound of steel on steel.

Clay let out a gasp of pain and his dagger clattered to the ground. He jumped back out of Arthur's range and shook his arm. He went from recovering from the blow to rushing back in toward Arthur. This time Arthur wasn't fast enough and took the punch in the side.

His whole body folded from the impact.

As he was straightening from the blow he brought his elbow up and caught Clay in his exposed face. The knight staggered back, eyes watering and blood pouring from what, a moment before, had been a nose.

The two continued to exchange blows while I ignored Arthur's request and watched everything with wide eyes.

I'd originally thought that Arthur would have the upper hand since he had a sword and Clay no longer even held a weapon, but Clay was fast, even in his armor, and he kept moving closer so Arthur couldn't use his sword to its full effect.

They were both tiring, though, I could see that. Clay from moving so much in what was obviously heavy armor, and Arthur looked like he hadn't rested in a very long time.

I had to help. I picked up my spear again and, with an angry shout, charged toward the two men.

I managed to aim well enough that my spear connected

with Clay—I'd almost been afraid I'd hit Arthur—and while I didn't manage to cut through his armor like I'd hoped, he did stumble forward.

He let out a small gasp of surprise and glanced over his shoulder to glare at me.

Arthur stepped to the side, allowing Clay to fall partially past him, then he raised his sword and drove the point home through the open face of the helmet.

That was when I decided to close my eyes.

I huddled down on the floor, weapon forgotten, and covered my face with my hands.

A moment later, I felt Arthur's strong hands pick me up. He smelled awful, but I didn't care. I wrapped my arms around his neck and cried.

———

Arthur carried me outside and told me to open my eyes. When I did I was greeted by the happy, crying face of Hazel. She practically ripped me away from Arthur and swung me around.

"Sweetie, I want you to meet somebody." She skipped the few steps over to the massive orc woman who was watching the whole exchange with a curious expression. "This is Ryta."

"Hi," I said, still trying to bury myself in Hazel's shoulder.

"You must be the Goretusk girl."

I hid my face as I nodded. I hadn't had much luck revealing my name to people lately.

"Good family, the Goretusks. Hey, Arthur, good to see you made it out alive." I looked up to find she'd already moved on from me to Arthur."

The old man nodded.

"Are you okay, sweetie?" Hazel asked me, interrupting my eavesdropping on the other conversation going on.

I nodded, managing to hold back the tears that wanted to escape.

"How long do you think before the city watch shows up?" Ryta asked.

"Not long," Arthur answered.

Hazel studied my face as I watched Ryta and Arthur talk.

"How do you two know each other?" Arthur asked.

Ryta laughed and walked back to Hazel. She threw an arm around the woman and ruffled my hair. "Hazel here is my wife."

Arthur stared at the two for a moment then laughed. "No wonder you were so desperate to get in here, Hazel."

Hazel and I stared at him in shock. I was pretty sure I'd never heard him laugh.

"That's right. Little lady can't live without me." The two laughed together.

They laughed longer than I felt was necessary, but at some point, both Hazel and I joined in. I didn't think any of it was funny, but it felt good to laugh.

Finally, Arthur took a deep breath and his face returned to its normal, serious expression.

"There's one more thing we have to do before this is all over."

"Um, mind if I ask what exactly happened here?" Hazel asked.

"A faction within the order was trying to resurrect Saban."

"That sounds bad," Ryta said. "Wait, resurrect? Wouldn't that mean—"

"He died ten years ago." He nodded at me. "Her uncle killed him."

"No shit?" Ryta gave me an admiring look. "But you stopped that, right?"

"Like I said, one more thing to do. Hazel, I'm going to need your help for this."

He led us across the temple grounds. I buried my face in Hazel's shoulder so I wouldn't have to look at the scenery.

She gently scratched my head as we went.

We stopped walking and I was passed up to someone else. I looked up to find Ryta's broken smile. She gave me a friendly wink then rested me on her shoulder. It felt safe there, and I grabbed a handful of her thick, black hair and watched Arthur and Hazel with her.

We were inside someone's home from the best I could tell. Arthur had pulled a book down from a bookcase and was flipping through it. He stopped at a page and handed the book to Hazel.

"I'm not sure which line it was, but—"

"I found it," Hazel interrupted.

She read the words out loud and both Ryta and I slapped hands over our ears to try and stop the pain.

"Now what?" she asked Arthur.

He took the book away from her and slid it back into the bookshelf. The shelf wavered, like a mirage, then vanished to reveal a doorway.

"Wait here. If I don't come back, burn the temple down. And," he stands in silence for a while, "Take care of the girl."

———

Arthur climbs down the stairs. He is tired. He does not feel drained like he did after Adrian had taken his power from him, but he is tired. A physical weariness that he hasn't felt in a long time. He hasn't been in a real battle in a while. That must be the cause.

For a while, he's not sure if he has the energy to climb down to the bottom of the steps, but he does.

He steps into the room to find Saban waiting.

The pit of tar is empty. He can see that it is only as deep as the wall. Knee high, at most. Sitting on the low wall is a man in a suit of armor blacker than even the ichor of the pit had been. Two eyes glow blue in the darkness of the helmet.

The figure is studying his hands. It turns the gauntlets over and over, inspecting every knuckle and groove in the metal.

Arthur approaches the figure. He has left his sword with Hazel and Ryta. He hopes he will not need it.

The dark helmet rises and the blue eyes consider Arthur. "Arthur?"

The deep voice that had penetrated Arthur's mind not long ago is gone.

"Saban." Arthur sits on the wall next to the armor.

"Am I Saban? I do not think I am."

"I don't think you are either."

"Then, why do I remember being Saban?"

Arthur shrugs.

"I can feel them, Arthur." The voice is hollow, emotionless, but Arthur senses the sadness in the words.

"Who?"

"All the people my knights killed. Their brothers...why would they do that?"

"They wanted to bring you back. They wanted your power again."

"Why would they think I would give them any of my power after what they have done?"

"It doesn't matter anymore. They're gone." Arthur studies his own hands and finds that they are shaking.

"I know. I can sense that too. There are so few left who have held my power."

"What happens now?" Arthur asks.

"I... I don't know. What do you think should happen now?"

"I don't think Saban should live again."

"Why?"

"I," Arthur takes a deep breath, "I don't know if this world needs him anymore."

"What about you?"

"I don't think I need him anymore."

"You haven't needed him for a long time, have you?"

Arthur is surprised by this question, but realizes he knows the answer. "I lived without him for twenty years. When he did finally come back into my life, he brought only death and misery."

"I don't remember his death."

"It wasn't much, as deaths go."

"How did it happen?"

"An orc. A warcrier."

"Ah. I remember them. Saban always feared the warcriers. I think he knew that was how he would die. It was either them or the Ki'mera."

"The Ki'mera?" Arthur does not know that word.

"He fled them. Centuries ago. It was how he ended up here. How *I* ended up here? When you left, Arthur, his—my—fear grew. You'd traveled worlds, just like them. What if they found him? Me?"

The armor grows silent.

For a long time the two of them sit, both alone with thoughts of fear and death and hatred.

"Arthur?"

"Yes?"

"Will you kill me?"

"I had considered it."

"No. Arthur, I am asking you to kill me."

"Oh." Arthur swallows. He has prepared himself for this, but now...now he does not know if he can.

"Here." The figure hands him a small blade. Its hilt and blade are blacker than a starless night. "It's all I was able to save of the wizard's magic."

"I see." As Arthur accepts the small weapon from the being that is not Saban, he is flooded again with the power of his dead god. He breathes in sharply at the sudden renewal of vitality.

They both rise and, without saying a word, they step over the wall into the small pool. They stop at its center and turn to face each other.

Arthur looks up at the imposing figure and wonders what it looks like underneath the armor.

"Please make it quick, Arthur."

"Of course." Arthur imbues the dagger with Saban's strength and drives the point of the blade through the neck of the figure. It parts the armor like the surface of a still pond. At that moment, without quite knowing why, Arthur touches the ever-flickering flame of Melody's magic and merges it with the torrent of Saban's.

Black sludge oozes from the wound and the armor deflates. The substance fills the pool, climbing up Arthur's legs, up to his knees.

Arthur closes his eyes and allows himself to sink once more.

EAST OF GLANZEND

ARTHUR HAD BEEN asleep for almost two days. Even as our cart bounced up and down along the dirt road, he did nothing but snore and occasionally murmur something in his sleep.

We'd found him at the bottom of the dark tower behind the bookcase and Ryta had carried him back up the stairs.

She and Hazel had refused to hand him over to the city guard when they finally arrived at the temple. An old knight named Victor had lectured the guards, insisting that Arthur was just another victim in a horrible coup led by Roderick Clay.

Apparently, the old man was a respected member of the order, back from before even Arthur had been a knight, so the guards listened to him.

He'd whispered something to Hazel and Ryta and handed them a bundled package. When I asked what he'd said they'd told me that they were taking me and Arthur away from the city.

I hadn't argued. I was a little sad I wouldn't get to see

Dederick again, but I didn't really like Glanzend too much. Not anymore.

We'd been on the road two days, and I'd spent almost every waking moment watching Arthur sleep. I would occasionally help Hazel mop up the sweat from his forehead, or gently pour water into his mouth, but mostly, I just watched him sleep.

Hazel and Ryta talked non-stop about their house. About the woods behind it and the herds of deer that would come and graze in the yard every night in the summer. About how I would make so many friends in their small community. A lot of orcs, Ryta assured me.

I said that sounded great, though I didn't mean it. I look more human than orc, and children are always surprisingly cruel about the little differences.

Hazel promised to teach me some magic if I wanted. I thought that would be great and told her so.

But mostly I just wanted Arthur to wake up.

I wanted him to teach me how to use a sword. Ryta said she could do that, "Goretusks are supposed to be great fighters, I'm sure you'll learn fast!" But I wanted Arthur to teach me. The way he moved without even trying. It seemed like the right way to do things.

It was after noon on the second day—I'd just finished the strip of dry meat and hunk of cheese that was my lunch —when Arthur sat up in the cart.

I almost didn't realize it at first, since I'd grown so used to him not moving I was sure it was just a trick of the light. I sat up straight, waking up from my own light slumber and gave a wordless shout.

Ryta stopped the cart and turned around to see what the commotion was about. "About damn time, old man."

Hazel lifted her head from Ryta's shoulder—a puddle of

drool was left behind—and gave her own surprised cry. "Arthur? How are you feeling?"

"Where..." He blinked his eyes a few times, trying to focus on us and the trees around us.

"Heading east out of Glanzend. About two days."

He grunted his understanding. "What happened? After I...you know?"

Hazel told him about the guards arriving and Victor vouching for him. "Miki, give him his pack, please."

I scrambled to the other end of the cart and picked up the parcel of fabric. "Here, this is from Mister Victor."

It was heavy, but I managed to waddle it the few steps over to him.

He took it and thanked me with a nod of his head.

He undid the knot that held it together and unwrapped it. Inside was a bundle of clothes. It didn't look like anything too special to me, but Arthur's eyes misted at the sight of them.

"What's that?" I asked.

"They're my old robes of office. Back before I was First Knight, I was the Master-in-Arms. I trained all the knights. Taught them how to..."

His voice broke and he put the items back. Next, he lifted a small satchel. He opened the bag and moved his hands around inside. He smiled fondly at whatever he saw inside. "He kept them after all these years."

"What?" I asked again.

"Just some old keepsakes." He pulled out a small blue stone carved in the shape of an eagle.

He returned it to the bag and closed it before picking up the last item.

It was a scabbard. A familiar sword hilt stuck out of it.

He drew the weapon. It was the same broken sword he had brought with him from Earth.

He smiled as he studied its length. His face grew contemplative as he lingered on the broken tip.

"Miki?" he asked.

"Yeah?" I said.

"What do you want to do?"

"What do you mean?"

"Do you still want to go home?"

I knelt and leaned in toward him, eyes wide. "Do you mean it?"

"Well...I don't know how yet. It's obvious I don't know anyone who can do it, but maybe we can find somebody?"

"Miki?" Hazel said.

Arthur and I looked at her.

"If you want, you know you can stay with Ryta and I as long as you want. You too, Arthur."

Arthur nodded. "If that's what Miki wants, then I will respect that. But, if you want, Mikaia, I will do everything in my power to find you a way home."

"I miss my mom," I announced. I realized it had been a long time since I'd even thought of home, but I did miss them.

"Then, we will get you back to her."

"How?" I asked.

"Well, let's find out. Together."

End of *Knights of the Dead God*

THANKS FOR READING!

Thank you so much for reading *Knights of the Dead God*. If you enjoyed the book, please consider leaving a review or telling your friends about Miki and Arthur's adventures.

Their adventure continues in the second Broken Redemption novel: *Gods of the Broken Sea*.

If you'd like to learn more about James Jakins and his books you can sign up for his newsletter here: http://eepurl.com/bHromb

ABOUT THE AUTHOR

James Jakins is a Fantasy Author. That's all that really matters, right?

He currently lives in Utah with his partner, and their dog and cats.